SHARLENE WATTS wondered how long she would be tormented for her tragic mistakes. Would she ever be able to face the consequences, or was she destined to continue running from the past?

RUSS MATTHEWS's heart had been broken too many times to give up Sharlene so easily. No matter what, he would build a life with her, one that would last forever. But could he ever resolve the turmoil threatening to tear them apart?

ANGIE PERINI vowed to do everything in her power to forget Willis. It had been a mistake to fall in love with him, to surrender to his passionate demands. But was she strong enough to resist his seductive charms?

Series Story Editor **Mary Ann Cooper** is America's foremost soap opera expert. She writes the nationally syndicated column *Speaking of Soaps*, is a major contributor to soap opera magazines, and has appeared on numerous radio and television talk shows.

Amanda Perkins is the author of several contemporary romances and an avid fan of ANOTHER WORLD. She lives and writes in Yonkers, New York.

From the editor's desk...

Dear Friend,

Captivating . . . exciting . . . heartwarming . . . these are but a few of the comments we've received from Soaps & Serials readers. We're delighted. Every month the fine team of writers and editors at Pioneer pool all their resources to bring you seven new spectacular books.

Based on actual scripts from ANOTHER WORLD, each novel is written with you in mind. Soaps & Serials take you back to the very beginning of the show, revealing the innocent and infamous pasts of your favorite characters, recreating cherished moments from your favorite episodes. And though each book is a complete, satisfying read, our sensational cliffhanger ending is just a hint of the drama that will unfold in next month's Soaps & Serials book.

We've recently received numerous requests for previous volumes of Soaps & Serials. If you are also curious about how it all began—or if you want to complete your collection—please see the order form inserted in this book.

For Soaps & Serials,

Rosalind Noonan

Rosalind Noonan
Editor-in-Chief
Pioneer Communications Network, Inc.

ANOTHER WORLD

12

LOVE
PLAY

Soaps™ & Serials

PIONEER COMMUNICATIONS NETWORK, INC.

Love Play

ANOTHER WORLD paperback novels are published
and distributed by Pioneer Communications Network, Inc.

SOAPS & SERIALS™ is a trademark of Pioneer
Communications Network, Inc.

ISBN: 1-55726-051-6

Printed in Canada

10 9 8 7 6 5 4 3 2 1

Mary Ann Remembers

ANOTHER WORLD

As you delve into Willis Frame's latest antics, your blood may begin to boil. You can thank Harding LeMay, the show's writer, for making you see red.

When LeMay began writing ANOTHER WORLD in 1971, he inherited the character of Steven Frame, a mysterious interloper who was the heartthrob of Bay City. In May of 1972, LeMay began creating a colorful background for him. It wasn't difficult. LeMay just dipped into his own past.

Born into poverty in northern New York State, LeMay was one of thirteen children. He ran away from home at the age of seventeen to become an actor and then turned to writing. So, one fine day Steve Frame confessed that he had left his indigent family to make his own way in the world, and that he had six brothers and six sisters.

As some of Steve's siblings—including dastardly Willis—surfaced in Bay City, LeMay went through a bit of a catharsis and wove more and more of his memories into the plot of ANOTHER WORLD.

Chapter One
The Cards Are Dealt

Angie Perini greeted the summons to Willis Frame's office with mixed emotions. Since throwing her aside for Carol Lamonte, he had treated her like any other Frame Enterprises employee: a nod when they passed in the corridor, a polite greeting when they found themselves sharing the elevator. Sometimes Angie thought she had dreamed the times they'd spent in each other's arms. But at night, when she was in bed alone, the memories haunted her so thoroughly, she knew those times had been real. All too real. All too unforgettable.

Angie picked up her stenographic pad and plucked two razor-sharp pencils from the mug on her desk. She straightened her charcoal-gray skirt, adjusted the hem of her royal-blue sweater around her trim hips, and marched down the hall, her businesslike demeanor belying her pounding heart.

She found the door to Willis's office open; he was pacing behind his desk, speaking emphatically into the telephone. Standing outside the door for a moment, she observed him. The impeccably groomed man in the gray pin-striped suit and red silk tie was not the Willis Frame she knew. She knew the weekend Willis, a man who wore jeans and flannel shirts, whose hair was tousled from walking in the wind, whose voice was full of laughter, whose eyes were bright with passion when they looked at her. This Willis—with his hard voice and dark eyes—was a stranger to her.

And just as well, she told herself. It would make her job that much easier.

She tapped lightly on the doorjamb. The sooner she started, the sooner she would be finished. Willis turned at the sound. His eyes scanned her deftly—her long dark hair, coal-dark eyes, compact well-proportioned body.

Angie bore up well under the scrutiny. It was the smile he turned on her that threw her. The feelings she had pushed aside seconds before surged through her. *Why can't I forget him?* she raged inwardly. For months she had tried to do little else, but it seemed a hopeless task.

"Come in, Angie," Willis said. "I'll be with you in a moment."

After walking across the vast expanse of carpet, she sat down in the chair opposite his desk. He said a few words into the phone and replaced it in the cradle. Hiking up a perfectly creased trouser leg, he perched himself on the edge of the broad mahogany desk. "How've you been?" he asked. "You're looking well."

"Thank you," she replied quietly, keeping her eyes fixed firmly on the sky outside the window.

"That color suits you. It's so bright it almost makes me forget this miserable weather."

Angie continued to stare out the window. Many stories below them, Bay City was a study in grays and blacks, huddled under a colorless January sky and bone-chilling winter rain. The weather was bad enough without engaging in small talk with Willis about it. Shifting her attention to the steno pad that was open and at the ready on her tightly clutched knees, she said, "I understood you had some dictation for me, Mr. Frame."

"Hey! What's this 'Mr. Frame' nonsense? You never used to call me that."

Angie stole a wary glance at Willis, and was greeted by an intimate smile. Against her will her heart started to leap, but she stopped it in midjump. She averted her gaze quickly. Willis Frame had hurt her very badly. She must not allow herself to forget that; she must not succumb to him again. "No, I never called you Mr. Frame before," she answered in a cold, steely voice, "but it seems appropriate now."

There was a moment's silence. She could feel his eyes still on her. Out of the corner of her eye she saw him stand and take a few steps toward her. Suddenly his hand was on her shoulder, burning her with its heat.

"I'm very sorry you feel that way, Angie. Very sorry."

She turned to look at him, unable to help herself. He was all contrition. Hope soared. Maybe he hadn't meant to hurt her, to be so callous. Maybe he was even sorry he had taken up with Carol. She smiled tentatively. "So am I, Willis."

He beamed at her. "That's better." He squeezed her shoulder and gave her a grateful, even submissive look that hid his true feeling of triumph. The last thing Willis needed now at Frame Enterprises was an enemy. Angie's furtive, damning looks had been bothering him. Her superb work put her in demand with all the executives, especially Vic Hastings, and he had to be sure not to drive her into Vic's corner. He hadn't been very tactful about dropping Angie for Carol, but there hadn't been time for finesse then. Carol was a very demanding woman. But now that Carol was securely his, he could afford to be conciliatory toward Angie. The way things had been going lately, he couldn't afford *not* to be conciliatory toward her.

Willis stepped back and leaned against his desk directly in front of her, his ankles crossed, his hands in his pockets. His manner was casual and friendly—not the least bit threatening. "Did you visit your family for Christmas? Was there one of those nonstop feasts you told me so much about?"

"Not an unbuttoned waistband in the house," Angie told him, pleased that he remembered her descriptions of her Italian immigrant family's holidays. Even when she was with him, she had never been quite sure that he was listening to her. He had always seemed so intent on his—on *their*—physical satisfaction. Though she had no one with whom to compare him, she was sure he was the most skillful of lovers.

"So Mama Perini really outdid herself this year?"

"I'm still dieting to make up for it."

"What for? Didn't I tell you before how well you're looking?"

"Yes, you did, Willis." There was a moment's silence. Angie thought she could hear her heart beating and spoke to cover the frantic pounding within. "Did you have a nice Christmas?"

"Well, things were a bit grim with the Frame clan," he said with just the right blend of dismay and male stoicism, a demand for sympathy, not pity. "Without Steve we're all at loose ends, especially Alice, of course. And I don't think Sharlene's ever gotten over losing her husband; you know that Joe died in Vietnam. Little Sally was a ray of sunshine, though. Precocious, that child, but charming. She's becoming more like Alice every day," Willis added, remembering to play on Angie's admiration for his sister-in-law.

"I'm sorry things weren't better for you," Angie said, wondering where Carol fit into the Christmas picture. Apparently, she'd done nothing to alleviate Willis's distressful family holiday, Angie thought with no little satisfaction.

"So am I," he said with regret and just a touch of longing. "But *c'est la vie,*" he said with a shrug. He straightened himself manfully and walked to the business side of his desk, where he picked up a sheaf of papers and leafed through them. "Now, about those letters. The first one is to Mr. George Rollins, Rollins Construction Company."

Angie's pencil rolled smoothly across the pad as he dictated a complicated set of figures and specifications. She was a crack stenographer and needed only half her attention to make a perfect transcription of Willis's words. The other half of her was thinking of the way Willis had looked at her, of the personal things he'd just said. She couldn't help but wonder if he had called her in that morning to begin making up with her. After all, Frame Enterprises was full of excellent stenographers. Any one of them—

"I need to talk to you immediately, Willis." Carol Lamonte's imperious voice shattered Angie's thoughts.

This is one time I'm not going to let her get to me, Angie vowed. Where was Carol when Willis needed her at Christmas? Angie would have loved to have been there, by his side, comforting him, doing her best to make up for the tragic loss of his brother. "I didn't catch that last number, Willis," she put in loudly. "Could you repeat it, please?"

Carol placed her elegantly suited body between Willis and Angie. "This can't wait," she said emphatically. She looked only at Willis, not giving Angie so much as a glance or a greeting.

"That'll be all for now," Willis said to Angie. His voice was cold, indifferent, and he didn't look at her, either. His eyes remained fastened on Carol.

"Shut the door behind you, Ms. Perini," Carol ordered.

Angie rose quickly and raced out of the room. How could she have been such a fool, to let herself think, even for a moment, that Willis might still be interested in her? It was over, and she had to forget him.

Shaking, close to tears, Angie sat at her desk, shoved a piece of paper into the typewriter, and started to bang at the keys, trying desperately to calm herself.

Neal Johnson watched the drama in Willis's office from a secluded spot in the corridor. When the door closed, he remained at his vantage point, pondering his next move. If Frame Enterprises hadn't been the only place in Bay City where a young architect could make his mark, he'd have marched into Willis's office and given him a piece of his mind. But there was no sense ruining his career because Willis had the manners of a barnyard rooster. Neal owed too great a debt to Robert Delaney, his mentor, who had hired him straight out of graduate school. Besides, if he had to leave Frame Enterprises, it would be impossible to make the drama end the way he thought it should: the villain and villainess unmasked, the fair lady wooed and won by the white knight.

Without benefit of a white-knight costume, Neal had been dating Angie for several weeks. She had never mentioned her affair with Willis, but it was not exactly top-secret information. In fact, when Willis tossed Angie aside for Carol Lamonte, the news had spread through the office like a prairie fire in August. Little else was whispered about over coffee breaks or in the company cafeteria. Neal had joined the company only a couple of months before Willis dumped Angie, and no one was happier than he was when the news broke.

Spotting Angie his first day on the job, Neal had been dismayed to hear she was Willis's steady date, but had ignored that fact with his customary aplomb. He had sized up the situation and befriended Angie. One meeting with Willis had assured him that Frame would move on to greener pastures the moment they appeared. When Angie's nights were no longer occupied, Neal had parlayed his casual friendship with her into a deeper relationship—deeper, but nowhere near the intimate, lasting bond he hoped to build with her. Not because he hadn't tried, however, but because Angie was still stuck on Willis. She might not have said it in so many words, but Neal knew.

He glared at the closed door to Willis's office,

angry that Willis could treat someone as good and uncalculating as Angie the way he did. But then, Willis was the type of man who assumed everyone operated on the same self-serving principles that he did. Neal also had to admit that he was becoming somewhat impatient with Angie himself. She was a smart woman. Why couldn't she see Willis for what he was? Why did she hang on to him?

He was getting annoyed with himself, too. Convincing Angie that he was the man for her was taking entirely too long. He'd have to step up his efforts, beginning right now.

Neal looked down the hall, spotted the coffee wagon and purchased two containers of coffee —black for himself, light and sweet for Angie. He'd bet a dollar that Willis didn't have the faintest idea how Angie took her coffee, or that she was a sucker for a raspberry jelly doughnut.

He carried the goodies to Angie's desk. She was pounding away so furiously that she didn't know he was there. "I thought you might need some midmorning sustenance," he said.

Angie brightened immediately at the sound of Neal's voice. He had a knack for showing up and raising her spirits whenever she felt down. When she turned to greet him and saw the treat he had brought, she smiled fondly. He certainly knew how to please her. "Thanks. Pull up a chair."

"Tough morning?" Neal asked as he sat down. He would never let on he had seen what had happened in Willis's office, but he wanted her to know that he was sensitive and sympathetic to her moods.

"Mmm," Angie said noncommittally through a mouthful of jelly doughnut.

"Well, don't get too frazzled. Save some energy for our date tonight, okay?"

"Don't worry. I will."

After chatting amiably for a few minutes, Neal rose to return to his office. As she turned back to her work, Angie realized she was feeling much calmer. The bitter aftertaste of her encounter with Willis and Carol had been replaced by a lingering sweetness. Why, she wondered, was she driving herself crazy over Willis when all she had to do was snap her fingers and Neal would come running?

The answer came all too easily. She had only to think of herself in Willis Frame's arms to know she could never feel the same way about any other man. No matter how sweet or kind or good he was.

Behind the closed door of his office, Willis shared his ample executive chair with Carol. When the time came, he would have to make her relinquish her job, but for the time being it was useful to have her as his right-hand woman. He brought his mouth down on hers again, letting his hand stray to the top button of her silk blouse. Unlike Angie, Carol did not surrender to him unconditionally. No, she feinted and parried, one excellent duelist pitting herself against another. The challenge to him was greater—but so was the reward.

Carol tore her mouth from his. "That's enough, Willis."

"It's never enough," he said with a laugh. He helped her from his lap and watched her straighten her claret red blouse and winter-white suit. Then he stood and tucked in a lock of the thick black hair that had fallen from the intricate knot on the back of her head. "There. Perfect again. What a team we make, eh, Carol?" He ran the back of his hand over her hot cheek.

She caught his hand and took it from her face. "That's right. A team. If one of us loses, we both lose."

"I'm well aware of the meaning of the word."

"Just making sure, darling." She reached up to straighten his collar and tie, and let her hands linger on his chest.

Willis stepped back and turned toward the window. "What else can I do for you?"

"Get rid of Sharlene."

"What do you want me to do? Drop my sister from the twentieth-floor window? Send her on a plane that gets lost over Australia like dear Steve's?"

"I want her transferred out of my office," she answered with exaggerated sweetness. "I feel as if she's always watching me, counting how many breaths I take. And I think she may have an inkling about our special project. She barged in this morning when I was on the telephone—"

"It's better to have Sharlene where we can keep an eye on her," he broke in.

"Then have her in your office," Carol retorted. "For heaven's sake, she lives with Alice. All she has to do is pass one casual comment over dinner and the whole project could go down the tubes."

"Carol, my love," he said coolly, "Sharlene will be very careful about what she says to Alice."

"How do you know that?" she demanded. Willis had as much at stake as she did. He knew they had to keep their special project a secret from Alice and her henchman, Vic Hastings. How could Willis be so sure Sharlene wouldn't tell Alice anything she knew? "You must know something that will guarantee Sharlene's silence," she guessed. "Don't you?" she prodded when he didn't answer.

"I know that she is my loyal sister. I'll mention to her that you'd like a bit more privacy in the office. I'm sure she'll understand. Now, why don't you run along? Who knows what people will start thinking if my door stays closed much longer?"

Carol raised her face for Willis's kiss. "They already think it, darling. I'll expect you at eight-thirty. Don't keep me waiting."

Willis kept his eyes on Carol's svelte figure and long slim legs as she walked out of the room. *Women,* he thought. How was he ever going to take over Frame Enterprises if he had to spend all his time pacifying women? He'd have to have a little talk with Sharlene before he got back to the Rollins job.

There was definitely something going on around there, Sharlene Watts thought as she sat at her desk in Carol's suite of offices—something Carol didn't want her to know about. There were too many mysterious phone calls on Carol's private line, and Sharlene was sure someone had been using her typewriter after hours. It couldn't be the two draftsmen who worked in the cubbyholes behind her desk. They always left before Sharlene did, and they didn't have their own keys to let themselves back in after everyone was gone.

Carol was the only one with access to the suite at night, but Sharlene couldn't imagine her doing her own typing. Carol refused on principle to do anything menial. Still, it must have been Carol who was using her typewriter, changing the margins and the tab settings. Sharlene had been through Carol's desk and all the unlocked office files and had found nothing unusual. She would have gone through the locked file, too, but she couldn't find the key.

Whatever was going on, Carol was more than likely to be in cahoots with Willis. Sharlene felt sure she'd be able to find some evidence in his office—he'd always been sloppy and careless. But there was no way Sharlene could go into his office. She might as well let herself unarmed into a hungry lion's den.

Even as she thought that, she heard the roar of Willis's hello. She crossed her fingers, hoping he would go right through into Carol's office. But no such luck. He passed the time of day with the draftsmen and then ambled over to Sharlene's desk. "Hiya, sis!" He leaned over and dropped a kiss on her cheek.

Sharlene recoiled at his touch. It made her feel soiled and dirty.

Willis ignored her silence. "Some weather, eh? Makes you want to hop on a plane and go someplace warm and sunny. Like San Diego. I always loved docking in San Diego when I was in the Navy. What a place! The zoo, the waterfront. The bars." He let out a long low whistle. "Those bars were something else. And sleazy! Let me tell you. I saw some things I wouldn't have believed if I hadn't seen them with my own eyes."

Sharlene tried vainly to keep the panic out of her face. This wasn't the first time Willis had mentioned San Diego to her in an insinuating way. He must have learned what happened to her in San Diego, or he wouldn't be bringing it up every time he saw her. But how could he know? How could he have found her?

"We'll have to chew the fat about San Diego sometime, sis," Willis was saying. "There's one particular story I know you'll just love." He patted her cheek roughly and headed for Carol's private office. "Catch you later."

She wanted to race across the room and pummel Willis with her fists. If only she had the courage to confront him, to find out how much —if anything—he really knew. But every time she thought about it she was stopped by thoughts of her fiancé, Russ Matthews. If Russ ever found out about San Diego, he would break their secret engagement.

How long, she railed, would she have to pay for her tragic mistake?

Chapter Two
Love Comes into Play

Angie left the office that afternoon at five on the dot. There was unfinished work on her desk, but she didn't care. She couldn't bear to be in the same building as Willis any longer. Outside, the icy rain stung her cheeks and soaked through her woolen hat and gloves, but she didn't mind. The cold was a relief after the suffocating atmosphere inside.

In her apartment, she hung up her wet outdoor gear in the bathroom and stripped off the clothes she'd worn to work. She tossed the royal-blue sweater aside. She would give it to one of her many cousins. Wearing it again would only remind her of Willis, and she had vowed to do everything in her power to forget him. It had been a mistake to have fallen in love with him, to have surrendered to his passionate demands. Tonight she would make a real effort with Neal.

After a reviving hot shower, Angie dressed in a

22

pair of black watch-plaid slacks and a white cowl-neck sweater. She put the television news on for company and scanned the movie listings in the morning paper to see what was playing. Neal rang the bell at five minutes to seven, early as usual. As she went to open the door, she thought involuntarily of all the times she had waited for Willis to pick her up, hours and hours of waiting if she added up all the times he'd been late. Well, those days were over, she vowed. With a fresh, welcoming smile on her face, she opened the door.

"Hello, Angie." Neal's strong open face wore a broad grin. Beads of melted ice were rolling off his light brown hair and over his cheeks to drop off his chin. "A bit damp out there tonight." He mopped his face with the back of one hand. The other remained behind his back.

"So I noticed. Please come in."

"Are you sure you want me to? I had to park half a block away and I'm soaked."

"All the more reason to come in and warm yourself up." He really was considerate, Angie thought as she motioned him in.

He shook himself off like a wet dog, wiped his feet on the mat, and came into the apartment. From behind his back he produced a paper cone of flowers. "For you, *signorina,*" he said with a small bow.

"Why, thank you," Angie replied, especially touched by his thoughtfulness tonight. She tore away the paper to find a bright bunch of red and violet anemones. "They're beautiful, Neal. The perfect antidote for the winter doldrums."

"Just what I thought. And they're your colors, Angie—striking, intense." As he spoke, Neal's gaze bore into her own.

Flushing slightly under his intent scrutiny, she averted her eyes, then hurried into her tiny pullman kitchen and busied herself finding a vase for her flowers. "Take your coat off, Neal. Can I get you a glass of wine?"

"I don't know if I should get too comfortable. I might not want to go out again. It really is miserable out there. If you'd rather not go—"

"Nonsense," she interrupted. The last thing she wanted to do was stay home alone tonight. "A little weather never hurt anyone. I won't melt."

"But I may," Neal murmured under his breath as Angie turned on the tap to fill the vase. "Then, let's get going," he said aloud when she turned the water off. "I'll get the car and pick you up in front of the building."

"There's no need for that," she told him as she came out of the kitchen. She put the flowers on her small gate-legged dining table and pointed to her sensible boots. "I've got a heavy coat, too."

"You're such a good sport, Angie. That's one of the many, many things I like about you."

And you're a good sport, too, Angie thought as she bundled herself into coat, hat, and gloves. He must have known about her and Willis, but he never once mentioned it. He never questioned or probed, never hit any of Angie's sore spots, never said anything unkind about Willis, even in an offhand way. Now that she was opening herself up to him, Angie was beginning to realize what a gem Neal really was.

They hurried through the freezing rain to Neal's car and drove slowly to Bay City's best pizzeria. They settled themselves at a cozy table in a corner of the near-empty restaurant, where they could watch the pizza maker tossing dough in the air and see the steam rise from the brick ovens where the pizzas were baking.

"Talk about bringing coals to Newcastle," Neal said. "I bet you got much better pizza at home."

"Not really," Angie assured him. "My mother doesn't have a brick oven. Or one of those wooden paddles with the long handles. That makes all the difference."

Suddenly Neal reached across the table for her hand. "And you make all the difference to me, Angie. To my life."

He looked away, embarrassed by his clumsy speech. But there was something about seeing her across the table, knowing he wanted to sit opposite her every night of his life that had made the words burst out of him. Then he noticed that Angie had not withdrawn her hand from his, hadn't flinched as she often did when he touched her.

"That slipped out," he said quietly. "I'm sorry."

"Don't be."

"Really?" he asked, his eyes searching her features.

"Really."

"I'm getting pretty crazy about you, Angie."

"I kind of thought you might be."

"And you don't mind?"

"No, I don't." And she didn't. Being with Neal made her feel secure, protected, cared for. Those were good feelings, feelings she shouldn't toss aside just because— Angie stopped her thoughts right there. She was not going to let Willis become an unwelcome third party on this date.

Over red wine and a pizza with sausage and mushrooms, Angie and Neal talked and talked —about the old house Neal was restoring and renovating, about his teaching Angie how to ski, about her teaching Neal to cook, about politics and current events, and whether it's possible for someone who's tone deaf to play a kazoo. By the time they left the pizzeria they were warm, inside and out, in mind and heart. The icy rain didn't seem so cold anymore.

Neal held Angie's hand throughout the film, caressing it, bringing it to his lips once or twice when they shared a laugh. After a tender, touching moment on screen, Angie, without even thinking about it, let her head drop onto Neal's shoulder. When she realized what she had done she fought an impulse to sit bolt upright and snatch her hand from Neal's. Instead she let herself relax into him, let herself feel the warmth and strength of him. She felt his lips brush the top of her head and she tried to savor and enjoy the moment. She very nearly succeeded.

After the movie, Angie invited Neal in for coffee. Sitting together on the sofa, they chatted about the movie for a time and then lapsed into a silence filled with many unspoken thoughts.

Neal was thinking how different Angie seemed tonight, more easygoing, happier to be with him. The guard that was usually on duty when they were together had been given the night off. He wondered if he should take advantage of such a timely absence.

Angie's mind was on how much she had enjoyed the evening. She could see herself spending many such evenings with Neal.

"Angie?"

"Mmm?" she replied.

"It was different tonight. With us, I mean."

"Yes, it was."

"I liked it. Very much."

"So did I, Neal."

Neal looked at her for a moment, overcome by a wave of longing and desire. He wrapped his arms around her and pressed his lips against hers. He felt her resist him for an instant, but then suddenly she melted against him, threw her arms around him, and kissed him as deeply as he was kissing her. Neal raked his hands through her hair, then pressed her body tightly to his. The kiss went on until they were both breathless.

"Angie. My angel," he murmured on ragged snatches of breath.

She held his head against her pounding heart. She had been afraid she would not respond to him, but she had. She smiled to herself and stroked his hair, wondering at the possibilities that were opening up for her that night.

Neal pulled away and sat up. "I'd better go now. If I kiss you again, I won't be able to leave."

"That's fair warning," Angie said, standing up. She was not going to rush things, the way she had done with— The way she had done before, she amended.

Neal picked up his coat and brushed his lips lightly against her cheek. "See you in the morning, Angie Angel," he said and was gone.

As soon as she had shut the door behind him, Angie felt a chill rise in her body. She had hoped, even expected, that his warmth would linger with her. But it was gone. *Give yourself a chance with him,* she told herself as she got ready for bed. *You can't expect everything to happen in one night. Next time it will be better.*

But she wasn't at all sure it would be.

"We shouldn't have to come all the way out here on a night like this to see each other, Sharlene." Russ Matthews looked at his fiancée's delicate face, paler than usual in the candlelight. At least he hoped it was the candlelight that was giving her such a ghostly look. A pang of love grabbed at his heart. "I love you, Sharlene. I want to tell the whole world—put signs up all over town, hire a plane to write it in the sky. As it is, I can't even tell my own sister."

"I need some time, Russ," Sharlene replied. "Time to settle things in my own mind. I haven't been a widow that long. I can't rush right into another marriage."

Russ pushed aside his dessert plate, with its barely touched slice of chocolate cake. His usually healthy appetite had deserted him tonight. From the moment Sharlene had arrived it was clear something was bothering her. She hardly said a word all night. Russ had had to keep the conversation going with talk of his heart patients and hospital gossip, but it had been uphill all the way.

"I don't think it's Joe," Russ said, his voice more even than his emotions. "I know it was hard for you—losing him in Vietnam, finding out about it just when you were supposed to meet him on leave in San Diego."

Sharlene flinched and turned her head away sharply.

Russ reached for her hand. "What's the matter, sweetheart?"

"Nothing," she said quickly, too quickly.

"Well, I think there is something wrong," he declared. "You're pale, jumpy, you didn't eat enough to keep a bird alive. Tell me. You have to trust me. Our marriage won't work if you don't trust me." He lowered his voice. "I've learned that the hard way."

"My poor Russ." Sharlene touched her hand to his cheek. "I haven't been very good company, have I? I'm sorry."

Russ took her hand and kissed her fingertips. "It's okay, Sharlene. But, please, tell me why."

Sharlene hesitated for a moment. Maybe she should tell him, she thought briefly, but then a cold wave of fear washed over her. What if she lost him? She wouldn't be able to bear it, she thought with a shiver. She gave what she hoped was a dismissive wave of her hand. "I'm just a moody so-and-so. I guess you ought to find that out before the wedding rather than after."

Russ heaved a sigh. "At least you're still going to marry me. I was beginning to think you might want to call off the wedding."

"Oh, no, Russ," she assured him. "I do want to marry you. Very much."

She fell silent, and Russ could feel her slipping away from him, into the distant, distracted state he'd noticed a few times before. He was determined to keep her with him. "How much time will you need? A week? A month? Six months? I'd like to have some idea, Sharlene, so I can plan. There are so many things to think about—a place to live, the ceremony itself, our honeymoon."

She didn't answer immediately, so Russ kept talking, trying to keep the mood light. "I know you can't tell me exactly: 'Well, Russ, I'll be ready to marry you in two weeks, three days, four hours, twenty-six minutes, and eight seconds.'" That raised a smile from her and Russ was heartened. "But if you could give me a ballpark figure—say to the nearest week—I'd be a very happy man."

Tell him about it, a tiny but insistent voice repeated in Sharlene's head. "What would you do," she began timidly, "if you found out something terrible about me?"

Russ looked at her, puzzled. "What do you mean, terrible?"

"Say I had some awful disease or—"

"If I couldn't cure you myself, I'd take you to the best doctors I could find, no matter where—" Russ stopped short. An image of Cindy Clark floated across his mind. He had already lost one woman he loved to a tragic illness. He would never let that happen again. "You must tell me," he said fiercely, "if you're not feeling well. We'll take care of it right this minute, Sharlene."

"I'm fine, Russ, really. I was just supposing."

"Are you sure? You must tell me the truth. Lying won't spare either of us."

Sharlene dropped her eyes quickly. "I'm perfectly well, Russ. Honestly."

He sought her eyes and looked into them deeply. "Promise me you'll never hide anything about your health. I couldn't bear it if I learned too late and couldn't help you."

"I promise," Sharlene said. She managed a

weak smile. "I'll call you at the first sign of a cold or a hangnail."

"Good. I'm glad we have that straightened out. I won't leave you if you're sick, Sharlene. The marriage vows say 'in sickness and in health.' I'll mean that when I say it. I mean it right this minute."

"You're so good to me." Impulsively Sharlene clutched his hand and held it against her cheek.

"That's because you're so easy to be good to." Russ lightly kissed her hand. "Now let's slay the rest of the dragons. What else are you afraid of?"

Sharlene gathered all her courage. Russ loved her so much. Maybe he would still love her if he knew the truth. "What if you found out I'd committed a terrible crime?"

Russ looked incredulous for a moment, then burst into loud laughter. "A crime? You? I can see the posters now. 'Baby-Face Sharlene Watts. Wanted for armed robbery in twenty-eight states.' What puts these silly ideas in your head, my love? The worst crime you're liable to commit is jaywalking. I think I could forgive you for that."

It had never occurred to Sharlene that Russ simply wouldn't believe she could have done anything wrong. If Willis did know what had happened in San Diego, *and* if he found out that she and Russ were engaged, *and* if he told Russ, Russ might simply dismiss him. That was an awful lot of *ifs*, especially when she didn't know what, if anything, Willis actually had seen in San Diego. She would be a fool to tell Russ about her past now. If it came up, she would deny it. After all, it would be Willis's word against hers.

"Now that we've dispensed with fatal illness and your life in crime," Russ was saying, "will you please tell me what's really bothering you?"

Sharlene folded her hands on the table. The icy feeling inside her had thawed a little, and she felt more secure about herself and Russ than she had in weeks. "I'm sorry. I don't know why I let myself get so upset about things. It's just something at work. One of Willis's intrigues—"

"Which twisted your stomach in knots," he broke in, "so you thought you were sick. And made you so angry you felt driven to seek vengeance. Am I right?"

She nodded, coloring at the lie.

Russ stroked Sharlene's reddened cheek tenderly. It was good to see some color in her face again. "Sharlene, my love, you have to stop worrying about things that will never happen."

"I know," she said softly. "I'll try."

"Don't just try. Do it."

She nodded and gave him a tentative smile. Outside, the rain beat a steady tattoo against the window beside their table.

"We'd better get going," Russ said after a while. "It hasn't let up out there, and I don't like your driving alone in this weather." He called for the check. As they waited, he kissed and caressed her hand and told her how happy they would be when they married.

It was so wonderful to see Russ content,

Sharlene thought. She had been right not to tell him. In the future she would have to be careful not to let Willis upset her.

Icy pellets of rain stung their cheeks as they raced to Sharlene's car. Russ climbed into the front seat with her, held her close, kissed her a dozen times, and told her just as often to be careful driving.

"Fussbudget," she teased, warm and flushed from his embrace.

"You're precious cargo," he said. "I want you to get home in one piece." He kissed her once more and reluctantly pulled away. "I'll call you tomorrow morning, after rounds."

"I'll count the minutes," she told him.

Sharlene drove home very carefully. She wanted to arrive safely, as tomorrow suddenly seemed very important. And the next day. And the next.

Chapter Three
Willis Plays His Trump Card

The sun was shining when Sharlene woke up the next morning. The winter-brown grass beneath her window still looked wet, but the sky was a clear, cloudless canopy. Although there was frost on the windowpane, the sun was already beginning to dissolve the feathery white streaks into colorless drops. She would do the same thing to Willis, she decided: melt the mist he had settled over her life into harmless water that would dry up and disappear.

She dressed in a bright suit of cherry-red wool and went down to breakfast. In the downstairs hall her sister-in-law was bundling her daughter, Sally, into a heavy winter coat.

"I'm only going from the door to the school bus," Sally protested as Alice pulled up the hood of the coat and wound a thick woolen scarf around her neck.

"It's cold out. I don't want you to get sick."

Sharlene smiled as she watched Sally lurch toward the door, stiff as a robot in her layers of clothing. "Good morning," she called.

"G'morning, Aunt Sharlene," came Sally's muffled voice from deep inside her coat.

Sharlene knelt down and sought her niece's face under the heavy hood and scarf. She'd hardly had time to peck the child's cheek when Sally broke away and raced out the door to the school bus standing at the door of the Frame mansion.

"Who was that masked girl?" Sharlene asked as the bus was lumbering down the driveway.

"Isn't she wonderful?" Alice asked with a doting smile. "I only wish—" She cut herself short. She had to stop wishing, every time Sally did something, that Steve could be there to share it. "Don't you look nice this morning," she said to Sharlene. "That color is lovely."

Alice was always so kind, Sharlene thought. She knew how hard Alice had taken it when Steve's plane had crashed, how hard it was for her to carry on without him, and yet she always had a good word for everyone. "Thank you," Sharlene said. "A morning this beautiful deserves something festive."

Alice looked down at her businesslike navy-blue dress, so correct, so drab. "I wish I'd thought of that when I dressed this morning."

"It's not too late to change."

Alice smiled, thinking that Sharlene's remark could mean more than just the dress she was wearing. She would have to try harder to finally accept that Steve was gone and get on with her life.

As they walked together into the dining room, Sharlene thought how right she had been to refuse to help Willis dissuade Alice from taking a more active role at Frame Enterprises. That decision had made an enemy of Willis, but she could never have betrayed Alice. If Alice hadn't offered her a place to stay, who knows where she would be now. She was glad that Alice would one day be her double sister-in-law. She would have to work hard on making that day arrive soon, so she could tell her the good news.

Thinking about Alice strengthened her desire to settle things with Willis once and for all. He had never said what he knew—or what he *thought* he knew—about her life in San Diego. Nor did he know that she was engaged to Russ. Why should she let Willis push her into a corner? He could be bluffing, after all. He had been known to do that. Frequently.

Sharlene helped herself to scrambled eggs and bacon from the covered dishes on the sideboard. Beneath the folds of a crisp linen napkin she found a basketful of cranberry muffins, still warm from the oven. Alice kept such a beautiful home, she thought as she sat at the table. Sharlene hoped she would be able to do the same for Russ. She had hardly had a chance with Joe; her life with him had ended all too quickly, and then . . .

Alice poured coffee from a gleaming silver pot into Sharlene's cup and then freshened her own half-empty cup.

"Thank you," Sharlene said, resolutely pushing aside the grim thoughts that pressed on her mind. Impulsively she reached out and touched Alice's hand. "Thank you for everything. You're so good to me. I haven't told you nearly enough how grateful I am to you for letting me stay in your home."

"You're Steve's sister, Sharlene. My home is your home. Anyone would have done the same. There's nothing to be grateful for."

"Yes, there is, Alice. A lot of people would have taken in a sister-in-law out of duty, but you've made me so welcome. I feel like part of the family."

"You *are* part of the family."

"Only because you've helped make me part of it again."

Alice's blue eyes began to fill, and she blinked away the tears. "I know how hard it is when you lose someone you love," she said, squeezing Sharlene's hand. "It's been a help to me, too, having you here. Now eat your breakfast before it gets cold, and before we both start bawling."

"Yes, ma'am," Sharlene answered with a smile and a crisp salute. Then, suddenly feeling very hungry, she concentrated on her breakfast.

After the meal, Sharlene and Alice went to

Frame Enterprises together. Outside Alice's office Sharlene gave her sister-in-law a peck on the cheek. "See you later," she said.

"Will you be home for dinner?"

"I don't have any other plans," Sharlene answered, and set off down the hall. She headed straight for her brother's office, and walked right in without knocking.

Willis and Carol were huddled over his desk, studying a set of blueprints. He looked up and glared at her. "What the devil—" he began angrily. Carol started to roll up the plans, but one of the large sheets fell to the floor. Sharlene tried to read the heading at the top of the paper, but it was upside down. Carol snatched it up quickly, and all Sharlene could make out was the first two letters of the first word: "Ja," or maybe "Jo."

As Carol fumbled with the plans, Willis lit into Sharlene, but he didn't attack her directly. Sharlene knew all too well that Willis didn't do anything in a straightforward way if he could find a better, more painful angle. She listened as he addressed his remarks to Carol, the better to ignore and hurt his sister. But she was determined not to let him get the upper hand and weathered his sarcastic speech as stoically as she could.

"I'll have to apologize for my sister," Willis said. "I thought she'd have acquired some manners, living up there in the big house with Alice Blue Gown, but I guess it'll take more than a few months of gracious living to make her forget that she grew up on the wrong side of the tracks."

"I'd like to speak to my brother alone, Carol," Sharlene said evenly.

Carol looked to Willis and he waved her away. "We can finish this later." When she had left, he gave a bored, weary sigh. "What is it, Sharlene?"

"I know you and Carol are up to something." She shook her head. "When are you going to grow up? You're acting just like you did as a kid, stealing Steve's stuff and trying to pretend it was yours. Well, now Steve's dead. You don't have to compete with him anymore."

"Just because Steve is dead doesn't mean I have to roll over like a good dog and let Miss Goody-Two-Shoes run Frame Enterprises like a Sunday school class."

"Frame Enterprises is Alice's to run as she sees fit. She doesn't wish you any harm, despite what you've done to her. Why don't you just leave it alone? What are you looking for, anyway? You've got a fancy office and a fancy salary to go with it. You live in a luxurious apartment; you can afford anything you want. You've got a classy girlfriend. How come it isn't enough? If you can't have any respect for Steve's widow, why can't you have some respect for our brother's memory?" Sharlene knew she wasn't getting through to Willis. Her words seemed to ricochet off him, but she had to fire a few more rounds. "Steve was so good to us. There were plenty of times that we wouldn't have eaten if it weren't for him, plenty of times he saved all of our butts."

A slow grin lit up Willis's face. "If Steve was such a great brother," he said in soft, measured words, "how come he couldn't keep you from becoming a prostitute?"

Sharlene felt as if she had been slapped. Her senses reeling, she struggled to stay upright, to find her voice. "What are you talking about?"

"I'm talking about this bar in San Diego, a dive called Georgia's, popularly known as the Bilge aboard many ships of the U.S. Navy. Thoughts of a blowout at the Bilge got many a lonely sailor through the long nights at sea—this lonely sailor included. I had never been to the Bilge, but my buddies told me all about it. A real down-and-dirty place. Liquor, women, drugs, gambling, fights. Whatever your pleasure, the Bilge had it. So what was the first thing I did when I got my liberty in San Diego? I headed for the Bilge." He paused for effect before continuing.

"And what do you think was the first thing I saw? A woman, talking to a sailor from my ship, a good buddy of mine. They seemed to be conducting a business negotiation. They argued a little, and the woman started to walk away. The sailor caught her arm and said something else. She smiled—a cold, hard, calculating smile—and held out her hand. He dug deep into his pocket and counted out several bills. Then she put her arm through his and they went through a door at the back of the bar. Now, just who do you suppose that woman was, Sharlene?"

He can't know, Sharlene kept repeating to herself over and over. *He couldn't have seen me. He's making all this up.*

But the longer Willis talked, the more Sharlene knew he wasn't bluffing. Willis had seen her at Georgia's, had seen her turning a trick.

"You didn't answer my question, sister dear. Who do you suppose that woman was?"

Sharlene kept her head down. She had no voice to answer. Besides, what could she say?

"It was you, Sharlene. My poor bereaved sister, so grieved by her husband's sudden and untimely death that it sent her into the arms of another man. Hundreds of other men."

Unwittingly Willis had hit upon the reason for those mad months in San Diego. "That's right," she heard herself say stonily. "It was so awful finding out that Joe was never coming home. I felt responsible, I felt as if it had been my fault somehow. I wanted to punish myself. I started drinking. I started seeing other men. One night, one of them got the wrong idea and gave me some money afterward. I kept it. And I accepted it from the next one, and the next, and before I knew it . . ."

"Please," Willis said acidly, "spare me the gory details."

"No, Willis, I want you to know why, I want you to understand what happened to me, how I sunk so low. Because if you know, you'll never tell anyone about what you saw. You'll forget it, just like I'm trying to forget it."

"I'm afraid I don't have as short a memory as you do." Willis sat down behind his desk, opened a file, and began to read.

The callousness of his action enraged Sharlene. She raced to the desk and pushed the file to the floor with a sweep of her hand. She fought against the tears that were burning behind her eyes, but as she spoke the sobs broke through the fragile barrier of her control. "You listen to me, Willis Frame. I am your sister, and I was once in very bad trouble, but that doesn't make me—"

"Oh, yes it does, sister." With slow, deliberate motions Willis reached down and picked up the file. As he spoke, he carefully rearranged the papers. "And save your tears for Russ Matthews. You're going to need them."

At the sound of Russ's name, Sharlene made a desperate attempt to calm herself. She choked out the words, "What's Russ got to do with this?"

"I should think your fiancé would want to know who he was marrying. It would be my brotherly duty to tell him about my sister's unfortunate path, wouldn't it?"

Sharlene's voice turned rock hard. Her face, her entire body felt carved out of stone. "As low as I sank, I was never as low as you are. I never hurt anyone except myself. But you, you don't care who you hurt, as long as you get what you want. How did you find out about me and Russ? What do you want from me?"

"Never mind how I found out about you and Russ. The important thing is that I know, and that Russ will know what I know, whenever I choose to tell him."

"He won't believe you," she said flatly. "It's your word against mine. Russ loves me and everyone knows you're a scheming, selfish son of a—"

"Please, Sharlene, watch your language in the office," he said smugly, turning his attention to the top paper in the file. Then he calmly began reciting his instructions. "I'd like you to talk to Alice tonight, and for as many nights as it takes, about how Steve would want her at home to take care of Sally, and how he would want me to be running Frame Enterprises. When and if Alice gives up her office here and fires Vic Hastings, I may suffer an uncharacteristic lapse of memory. Run along now. You're late for work and I'm very busy."

She pulled herself up and looked straight at Willis, even though he refused to meet her gaze. "I won't do that," she said, summoning every ounce of her courage.

"I see." Willis reached for the telephone. "I can reach Russ at Bay City General, can't I?"

"No," Sharlene screamed. "Don't. Please, Willis."

Willis put down the phone. "All you have to do is say a few words to Alice, and my lips are sealed."

"All right," she whispered. Broken, defeated, she limped from the room and continued on out the door of Frame Enterprises. In a daze, she wandered the streets of Bay City, not knowing what to do or where to go.

Several hours later, Sharlene found herself in front of the Madison Hotel. There was a taxi in the rank by the door. "The airport, please," she said as she got in. Her voice sounded normal, even above the ringing in her ears.

As the cab sped off, her head seemed to empty; the horrible stuffiness was gone, the pounding inside stopped. In that first quiet moment she realized she had made her decision. She was going home. To Chadwell. To Emma.

At the airport she took the first plane out of Bay City to St. Louis, then changed for a flight to Tulsa, Oklahoma. With the little cash she had left, she took a taxi to the bus station and got on the bus to Chadwell. She walked the last half mile to Emma's house.

She didn't have to think much about what she was doing during the trip. She seemed to be on automatic pilot. Her body was moving, but her mind was stuck in San Diego, reliving those long desperate months. The pain, the degradation, the humiliation of that time played in her head in vivid color. The more she remembered, the more she was convinced that Russ must never know. How could he love her, hold her, make love to her knowing that . . .

No, Russ must never know.

She mounted the steps of Emma's house and

raised her hand to knock on the door. Before her knuckles met the wood, the door flew open and there stood Emma.

"I couldn't believe my eyes!" Emma exclaimed. "I glanced out the window and I saw you coming up the path. I thought I must be seeing things, but it is you! Come in here, and give your big sister a hug."

Emma's arms folded around her, feeling to Sharlene as if she were being wrapped in a warm, comforting blanket. She let her head rest against Emma's shoulder and, her guard down, began sobbing. Emma held her tight and rocked her gently until the sobs subsided.

"Sharlene, honey, whatever is the matter?" Emma led her to the sofa and helped her out of her coat. "I want you to sit right here and tell me all about it. Everything."

Sharlene managed a wan smile and sank into the soft cushions.

Chapter Four
The Truth Denied

An emergency operation kept Dr. Russ Matthews at the hospital until late that afternoon. Still wearing his surgical greens, he telephoned Sharlene from the doctors' lounge. The news he received was disturbing. Sharlene hadn't been at her desk all day, and no one at Frame Enterprises had seen her since early that morning.

Russ showered quickly in the dressing room and then changed into his street clothes. He had left patients waiting in his downtown office when he got the emergency call, so he had to return there immediately.

He briefly debated whether or not he should phone Alice and ask after Sharlene, but he decided against it. Probably, Sharlene had gone home with a sore throat or a cold. Anyone could have picked up a bug after being out in the previous night's rain. Calling his sister would only worry Alice. Also, although Alice knew he and Sharlene had dated several times, she had no idea how serious their relationship had become; Russ wanted to avoid her becoming suspicious as it would be difficult for him to keep the engagement a secret if Alice had any inkling. He was bursting to tell someone the good news, and all he needed was a little encouragement.

The only thing he could think to do was call his sister and invite himself over for dinner. He called her before he left for his office and was duly issued a cordial invitation. *Mission accomplished,* he thought as he walked through the parking lot to his car. Now he would be able to see for himself that Sharlene was all right.

Russ arrived at the Frame mansion at seven and was ushered into the family room, where Sally and Alice were playing checkers.

Sally tore herself away from her game long enough to greet her uncle and extract a promise of a game from him. "There's time for one more before dinner," she told him.

Russ looked to Alice for confirmation. "Just one, Sally," Alice said with a nod as she held out a welcoming hand to her brother. Russ took her hand between both of his and kissed her soundly on the cheek. He stood by the table, absently watching the finish of the game, wondering where Sharlene was.

"You never could play checkers," he said to Alice as she made the move that allowed Sally to capture the last of her pieces.

Alice rose and offered Russ her seat. "Unlike you, who beat me every time when we were kids. Watch out for him, Sally. He plays a mean game of checkers. If you'll excuse me now, I'll pop into the kitchen to see how dinner's coming along. You must have known Mrs. Marsh was making your favorite when you called."

"Fried chicken? My radar must be working today," Russ said heartily. Alice's housekeeper did make delicious chicken, but he was more interested in Sharlene's whereabouts than what was for dinner. "Is Sharlene out tonight?" he asked, hoping he sounded casually polite. Alice's frown made him even more anxious than he already was.

"I was expecting her. We went to the office together this morning, and she said she'd be home for dinner. It's not like her to be so late and not call."

"Maybe she's working late," Russ suggested.

"That's what I thought, but when I called the office about half an hour ago, Carol said she wasn't there. What has me worried, though, is that Carol said she hadn't seen Sharlene since this morning."

"You don't suppose she was taken sick?" Russ remembered Sharlene's asking him what he'd do if he found out she was seriously ill. Maybe she really was ill. . . .

"No, if she'd felt unwell at work she'd have gone to the dispensary. If the nurse had sent her on to the hospital, she'd have notified someone upstairs—Carol, Willis, or me. I just don't understand it."

Russ felt a tug on his jacket sleeve. "Excuse me, Uncle Russ, but the board's all set up. If we don't start soon—"

"You two get on with your game," Alice said. "I'm sure Sharlene is fine." But she wasn't at all sure about that. Sharlene seemed to have been on an emotional roller coaster the last few weeks —up one day, down the next. Alice knew she had disappeared before, after Joe died, and had been vague about where she had been all those months. Alice was very concerned, but she made light of it with Russ. There was no reason for her brother to be burdened with Frame family problems.

Russ was so distracted by Sharlene's disappearance that he couldn't even play a decent game of checkers. Sally beat him so easily that she accused him of letting her win just because she was a kid. "I want to win fair and square," she admonished.

"You did win fair and square, Sally. I had a hard day at the hospital today and I'm very tired. I wasn't thinking clearly, so you'd better watch out the next time we play. I'm going to beat the socks off you."

Alice called them in to dinner then. Russ was aware of an empty spot inside him. Because of the emergency he'd missed lunch, but the gnawing sensation wasn't hunger. He ate distractedly,

barely tasting the food. Even Mrs. Marsh's coco-
nut layer cake couldn't make an impression on his
palate.

After the meal Alice took Sally upstairs to help
her get ready for bed. She left Russ in the family
room and asked him to start a fire. When she
came down, she promised, they'd have a good
long gossip.

Up in smoke, up in smoke. The refrain rattled in
his head as he laid the fire. Could it be possible
that another relationship was going up in smoke?
Why did it keep happening to him? he wondered.
Every time he fell in love with someone, the
future plans he would dream about would never
come to pass. Well, he wasn't going to let that
happen this time. No matter what, he would
marry Sharlene and build a life with her, one that
would last forever.

"Russ?" He started at the sound of Alice's
voice and turned around. "Welcome back," Alice
said. "You were a million miles away. When are
you going to learn to leave your patients at the
hospital?"

Russ stood as Alice walked to the couch in
front of the fire. "Talk about the pot calling the
kettle black. When you were nursing you were
the same way." They sat side by side and watched
the dancing blue flames for a moment.

"Sometimes I wish I were back at the hospital," Alice said with a sigh. "Looking back, it
seems so simple."

"Are you sure you're not doing too much? At

Frame Enterprises, I mean. You're not exactly cut out to be a hard-driving businesswoman."

"No, but I have to do it, Russ. The company was Steve's pride and joy, and I have to keep it going the way he would have wanted. If I'm not there to keep an eye on things, it won't be Steve's company anymore. You know what happened when I wasn't around. Willis is a very talented young man, but—"

"Willis is a pain in the neck," Russ broke in bluntly. "I'm sorry, but you married Steve, not his family."

"I don't feel that way at all. I have an obligation to maintain the relationships Steve would have had with his family. Would you have wanted me to turn Sharlene away when she needed me?"

"No, of course not. I'm not talking about Sharlene."

Alice reached out and touched her brother's hand. "I'm very worried about Sharlene. When I was upstairs I called Willis. He said she dropped into his office to say hello this morning and he hasn't seen her since. Do you think I should call the police? Maybe there was an accident." She started to get up.

"Just a minute," Russ said. "Don't you think that's a bit odd? Sharlene 'dropping in to say hello' to Willis. They're not exactly on the best of terms."

"No, they're not. Did Sharlene tell you that?" She couldn't remember ever mentioning to Russ that Willis and Sharlene weren't getting along. Of course, he knew that Willis had stepped out of line once or twice at the company, but how would he know about the friction between Willis and Sharlene? She had barely spoken to Sharlene herself about it. Alice was surprised that Sharlene would open up to Russ; her sister-in-law was always so secretive with her.

"Oh, well, yes. I guess Sharlene must have mentioned it the last time we went out."

"That's good that she opens up to you," Alice said thoughtfully. "She seems to have so much on her mind, and I've always been concerned that she keeps her troubles bottled up. I guess she figures I have enough problems of my own." Glancing at her watch, she added, "I do wish I knew where she was. I'm worried."

The sound of the telephone brought Russ and Alice to their feet in a single motion. "I'll get it," Alice said as she raced to the phone in the hall. "That has to be her."

It took all of Russ's willpower not to follow his sister into the hall. "Thank God you're all right," he heard Alice say. "We were getting so worried." There was a pause and Alice explained, "Russ is here." After that there was a series of "yeses," "buts," and "I sees." Alice asked several times for a phone number and finally he heard her repeat several numbers.

Alice was visibly relieved when she returned to the room. "That was Sharlene," she said.

"Where is she?" Russ asked as calmly as he

could, though he wanted to grab Alice's shoulders and shake every bit of information he could out of her.

"Well . . ." Alice hesitated. "She asked me not to tell anyone where she is. She just said that she had to get away suddenly and that she's all right and that she'll let me know when she'll come back. I don't know, Russ, she sounded very disturbed."

"What do you mean? Was she hurt? Sick?"

"No, I don't think so. She assured me she was all right. But she sounded very upset." Alice was silent for a moment. "I wish I could help her, but she's a grown woman. I can't force her to tell me anything she doesn't want to."

Just then a bloodcurdling scream came from upstairs. "Mommy! Mommy!" Sally yelled.

Alice blanched. "She must have had another nightmare," she said, bolting from the room.

As soon as Alice was up the stairs, Russ went into the hall. There was a pad and pen beside the phone, but the top page was blank. Alice must have put the paper with Sharlene's number somewhere else. He ran his sensitive fingers over the top sheet on the pad, feeling the impressions of the number Alice had just written. With the pen, he traced over the impressions until he could read the white numbers against the blue pen scratchings. He dialed the number quickly, and a woman answered. "This is Dr. Russell Matthews. I'd like to speak to Sharlene Watts, please."

"Just a minute, please," the woman replied. He

heard some muffled talking in the background while he waited. "You have the wrong number," she said when she returned to the phone. Before Russ could say anything else, the line went dead.

"I'll shelter you, I'll feed you, I'll love you, Sharlene, but that's the last time I'll lie for you," Emma said firmly. "Who is this Dr. Matthews? Any relation to Alice?"

"Alice's brother," Sharlene said faintly. "Alice said he was there. She wouldn't have given him the number after I asked her not to. He must have poked around and found it. I never should have given it to her, but I just wanted to get off the phone and I couldn't refuse Alice. She's been too good to me."

"So why would this Dr. Matthews go snooping through his sister's things in order to call you? Is he some kind of weirdo?"

Sharlene had to laugh. She couldn't imagine anyone less weird than Russ. "No," she admitted sheepishly. "He's my fiancé."

"Oh," Emma replied. "That makes it all clear —as mud." She poured herself a fresh cup of coffee and sat opposite her sister at the kitchen table. "Let me guess. Is he the reason I practically had to get a cattle prod before you'd call Alice to prevent her from worrying herself to death?"

"Indirectly." Sharlene leaned back in her chair and let her head loll back. Everything was such a mess. How was she ever going to fix it?

"Did you have a fight with him? Is that why

you ran away? Sharlene, honey, you can't run away every time something bad happens in life. Sooner or later you're going to have to stand and face things, and sooner or later you're going to have to start confiding in people. Lordy, I'm your own sister, and you never even let me know your husband died. You just disappeared in San Diego and we didn't hear from you for months."

Sharlene straightened her head. "I didn't disappear," she said softly. "I was in San Diego the whole time."

"Doing what, honey? Why didn't you let us know? I'd have come out to be with you, instead of your sitting alone, crying for months on end."

"I wish I had been sitting alone, crying."

"Instead of what?" Emma coaxed. "Tell me, honey. Tell me everything. It'll make you feel better."

Sharlene had never told a soul about her time in San Diego, but suddenly the whole story poured out of her. She couldn't carry the burden of secrecy anymore. She had to tell. She started at the beginning: waiting day after day in the cheap motel for Joe to arrive, then finding out he was dead.

She couldn't believe it at first. She kept waiting for him to show up. To pass the time, she started going to bars. She drank more and more, trying to numb the awful feelings inside her. It was her fault that Joe had died. She shouldn't have let him go to Vietnam. She should have made him run away to Canada or Sweden, like so many others were doing. But she let him go. She hated herself, as much as if she'd killed him herself.

One night she had so much to drink she got confused. A guy picked her up in the bar where she hung out, a place called Georgia's. He looked like Joe, he let her call him Joe, and in her mind she convinced herself it was Joe. She took him to her room. Again and again, the same thing happened. Then one night someone left twenty bucks on the night table. She needed the money as she hadn't cashed any of the checks from the Army; that was blood money to her. It didn't take long for the woman who ran Georgia's to figure out what she was doing, and she offered Sharlene a job in the operation she ran from behind the bar.

Emma said nothing, letting Sharlene talk it all out. She hid her own emotions—shock that such a thing could have happened to her very own sister, dismay that Sharlene had felt so alone she hadn't called her for help.

"After a few months," Sharlene was saying, "I woke up one morning and it hit me, what I had done to myself. So I took all the checks I had saved from the Army, put them in my purse, and walked out of that place. I checked into the best hotel in town and took about twenty-five showers. It was as if I couldn't get clean enough. Then I ordered a meal from room service—the first decent one I'd had since I found out about Joe—and finally I had the strength to cry. I cried for days. Then I went out, bought myself some new clothes, opened a bank account, and called Alice. The next day I was in Bay City."

Emma got up, put her arms around Sharlene, and held her close. "Sharlene, honey, I am so sorry, so very sorry."

"It wasn't your fault." Sharlene thought she had finished crying, but a fresh torrent of tears poured out.

"But I'm still so sorry for your trouble. You have to put all that behind you now. It's over. You pulled yourself up by your own bootstraps and you've got a new life to look forward to." She stepped back and handed Sharlene her handkerchief.

Sharlene wiped her face and looked up at her sister's strong, handsome face. "That's what *I* thought. Until Willis got involved. Oh, Emma, he knows. He saw me there, at Georgia's, and he's threatening to tell Russ." Emma sat down and Sharlene told her that whole long tale, about Willis's wanting to take over the company and trying to use her to get his way with Alice.

Emma could feel her face getting red as Sharlene spoke. That Willis! She'd never had much use for her younger brother, but this was too much. Willis had gotten away with too much in his life. He wasn't going to get away with ruining Sharlene's life or the company that Steve had worked so hard to build. "I'll tell you what we're going to do, Sharlene. We're going back to Bay City tomorrow. You're going to tell your fiancé the truth. That'll take the wind out of Willis's sails. Nothing will give me more pleasure than walking into that little weasel's office—"

"I can't," Sharlene said in a strained voice. "I can't tell Russ. I won't."

Emma tried to reason with Sharlene, but nothing she said made any difference. Finally she gave up—for the time being. "You're too tired to think clearly tonight, honey. It'll all look better in the morning, after a good night's sleep."

Emma ran a hot bath for Sharlene, put out a fresh flannel nightie for her, and sat with her until she fell into a restless sleep.

"We'll get this all straightened out," she whispered to Sharlene's sleeping form. "But you'll have to tell the truth, Sharlene. The truth is the only thing that can set you free. I hope I can get you to see that." She kissed her sister's forehead and quietly left the room.

Chapter Five
Cat and Mouse

Vic Hastings sat down on the sofa in Pam Sloane's apartment, stretching his long legs in front of him. Folding his arms behind his head, he watched contentedly as Pam prepared coffee in the tiny pullman kitchen across the room. It seemed that every day she revealed a new facet to him. Besides being beautiful, with her long chestnut waves and golden brown eyes, she was a great cook and a gracious hostess. Her apartment could have been featured in one of those magazine articles on how to create a fabulous living space on a shoestring. She was honest and direct, and she had a sense of humor and fun. When he had first noticed she was an efficient secretary, he hadn't expected to want to know anything else about her. But he had become intrigued enough to break one of his cardinal rules—the one about mixing his business with pleasure—and he very much liked what he had learned.

"That was a great meal," he said. "You are a woman of many and varied talents."

"Thank you, sir," Pam replied. The dinner had been more intimate and comfy than any of the many memorable evenings she had spent so far with Vic. She had made her mother's famous chicken fricassee and buttermilk biscuits, so her small city apartment had a homey country smell. A wood fire was the only thing missing; on her secretary's salary she couldn't afford an apartment with a working fireplace. Maybe she wouldn't be living alone on a secretary's salary for too much longer, though. She and Vic were getting very close, but she knew she shouldn't rush things, for either of them.

She put a dish of chocolates on the tray and carried it into the living room. Sitting on the edge of the sofa, she poured the coffee while Vic carefully chose a chocolate shaped like a beehive and bit into it. "Mmm."

"Chocolate-covered cherry," Pam stated with a smile. They were Vic's favorite, and he was always as pleased as a little boy when he picked one out. There were many moments, like this one, when she had a hard time remembering he was a high-powered executive at Frame Enterprises.

At work he seemed formidable: tall and elegant, with straight dark hair and gray eyes. He moved and acted with precision and decisiveness. He treated the staff kindly, never raised his voice, but at the same time commanded excellence and dedication. Pam had admired him long before they became involved outside of work.

Their relationship had started innocently enough. She had stayed after hours several evenings in a row to help Vic with a rush project. They worked well together. Pam could anticipate Vic's needs, and she fulfilled them unasked. She was organized, had a sharp eye for detail and a good memory, but the thing that made her a perfect ally for Vic was her unflappable disposition. Like him, she didn't get flustered under pressure, didn't make mistakes because she let herself get harried.

When the project had been completed, Vic invited her to dinner. To thank her for her work, he presented her with a handsome bonus. She had appreciated that a great deal, but the greater bonus was finding that they got along well outside the office, too. They began to see each other now and again in the evening and eventually on weekends. They had been careful not to let anyone in the office know about their personal relationship. Pam had been as adamant about that as Vic. She didn't want anyone pitying her the way they had pitied Angie after Willis had thrown her over for Carol. How Angie could show up for work every day after that was a mystery to Pam. She would never let something like that happen to her.

"You're awfully quiet," Vic said after finding and devouring a second chocolate-covered cherry.

"Sorry." Pam kicked off her loafers and stretched her legs out on the sofa. "I was just thinking how very glad I am that we've kept our private life private, instead of having everyone at the office blabbing about us behind our backs."

Vic patted her delicate ankle and gave a small laugh. "Funny, that's just what I was thinking. It's getting uncanny, the number of times we find ourselves on the same wavelength."

"Great minds think alike," Pam quoted with a grin.

"What would you say about putting your 'great mind' on a special project for me?"

"That depends on what it is."

Vic moved over, put his arms around Pam, and gave her a big hug. "That's what I like so much about you, Pam. You're always your own person." He sat back and took her hand in his, caressing it as he talked. "So many women would have agreed to do anything for a man, without even knowing what it was. But I know that if you don't want to do this you'll say no. That's why I can feel comfortable asking you."

"This is starting to sound interesting, as well as serious." She looked down at his hand: the long tapering fingers, the impeccably groomed nails. She liked the way it looked wrapped around her smaller, more delicate hand. They did make a good team, but Vic was right. She'd never do anything she didn't want to do, for him or anyone else. He had piqued her curiosity, though.

Vic dropped her hand and began to explain.

"Willis's sister appears to have taken an extended leave of absence—which seems a bit fishy in and of itself, but I'll get back to that. That leaves a vacancy in Carol Lamonte's office. I'd like to see that you fill that vacancy."

"Why? So you can have your own personal Mata Hari?"

"You do catch on quickly."

Pam turned her body to face Vic and folded her legs under her. "It doesn't take a genius to see that Willis is out to grab whatever he can. Of course, I wasn't privy to all the details, but I know there was some trouble with that shopping center project that he and Carol were working on a while back. And now that he and Carol are hand-in-glove—in more ways than one—I can see that it would be useful to you to have someone there to watch for, well, any unusual ripples in the pond, shall we say."

"That's it. I couldn't have said it better myself." He looked at her and shook his head.

"Great minds," Pam reminded him with a shrug. "But how are you going to make sure I get a transfer to Carol's office? Won't Carol or Willis be suspicious? Even though no one knows about our personal relationship, it's common knowledge at the office that we've worked closely together on a number of projects."

"Aha!" Vic crowed. "There is something you haven't mysteriously divined. I'm going to arrange to have the recommendation come from Harvey Blanchard."

"Mr. Blanchard? Isn't he awfully close to Willis?"

"So it would appear. But what Willis doesn't know is that Harvey reports back to me. I've let a few things supposedly slip by under my nose to reinforce Harvey's seeming loyalty to Willis."

"Boy!" Pam exclaimed. "Mata Haris, double agents. You're running a regular den of intrigue, Vic."

He grinned back at her, but soon turned serious again. "This job isn't without its risks," he warned. "If your cover's blown, there's only so much I can do to contain the damage."

Pam thought for a moment. If she didn't take some risks, she'd end up being an assistant all her life. Proving herself cool and capable in a volatile situation could do a lot toward getting her a management position. "I'll level with you. You know I don't want to spend my career in the secretarial pool. If I do a good job on this assignment, I want your assurance that you'll do whatever is necessary to get me a promotion."

Vic considered the proposition. Should anyone find out he had planted Pam in Carol's office, it might be easier to promote her out of the executive suite to a line management job. That way everyone would win. "You've got it," he agreed.

"Great!" This could be the break she'd been waiting for, Pam thought. Her folks might not have been able to pay for a fancy education, but they had taught her to ask straight out for what she wanted. She might not always get it, but it never hurt to ask. "Now, tell me about Sharlene," she said, getting back to the business at hand. If she were going to succeed, she needed as much information as possible.

"She more or less disappeared last week. First I heard she was sick, then I was told she'd taken an extended leave of absence. I talked to Alice about it, but she was very closemouthed. I know there's been some tension between Sharlene and Willis since that shopping center deal, but I'm not sure what it's about. It could be about the business; it could be some personal vendetta. I don't know. The whole situation puts a bad taste in my mouth."

Pam leaned over and put her head on Vic's shoulder. "Don't worry," she said. "Mata Hari Sloane will change sour to sweet."

Vic took her in his arms and brought his lips close to hers. "She always does," he whispered. His mouth sought her warm full lips and planted a deep lingering kiss on them. "My only regret," he murmured, "is that you and I will have to be extra careful. At least for a while. We can't take any chances on being seen together outside the office." He lifted her hair and nibbled at her soft delicious neck. "I am so sorry about that, my darling."

"So am I." Pam clung to him, savoring his caresses. "But we still have tonight."

He looked at her, his gray eyes cloudy with

passion. "Yes," he said softly. "The whole long, long night."

Later that week, Carol and Willis were relaxing after an intimate dinner at her elegant apartment. The setting—plush cream-colored carpet, mirrored walls, white leather furniture, glass-and-chrome tables—contrasted sharply with the rag rugs and patchwork quilts that Pam used to personalize her modest secondhand furnishings. The food had been *haute cuisine* as opposed to the down-home cooking Pam had served to Vic. But the conversation turned on the same topic that had occupied Pam and Vic on that earlier evening.

"Do you really think we can trust this Sloane person?" Carol asked Willis as she handed him a snifter of brandy. She sat next to him on the couch, arranged the folds of her dramatic violet caftan shot with gold, and crossed one knee over the other. "She seemed all right when I met her. Very bright and capable. Her record is impeccable. Perhaps too impeccable. After all, we—I mean you—don't have any hold on her. I know I didn't like having Sharlene around, but at least she was a known quantity."

She tapped her gold-slippered foot against the carpet while she waited for Willis to say something. The whole business made her edgy —Sharlene disappearing, having to break in a new secretary just when things were starting to happen on the secret project. The situation was delicate enough without unexpected problems cropping up.

"Stop worrying," Willis said blandly. "Harvey recommended her personally. That's good enough for me." He swirled the brandy in his glass, sniffed its bouquet, and took a long sip. Carol could be a trial at times.

"Hasn't she done a lot of work for Vic?"

"Some," he answered, controlling his temper. "She's also done a lot of work for Harvey and some for me. Her work is very good, and she's absolutely trustworthy, according to Harvey."

"And you trust Harvey implicitly?"

"Harvey's done a lot of favors for me, favors Vic would not be happy to know about. So will you *please* stop worrying? Everything is going to be all right."

"Well . . ." Carol hesitated. "If you're sure . . ."

Willis's temper finally got the better of him. "What's your problem, Carol? You're the one who's been bugging me about needing another secretary, telling me our project's going to fall through if you don't get some help. What do you want to do? Bring in someone from the outside who knows absolutely nothing about the way the company operates? That wouldn't do you much good, would it?" He took another long pull on his brandy, reminding himself that he needed Carol to pull off his coup. She had her uses, but sometimes she was entirely too timid.

"All right! You don't have to bite my head off."

Carol turned away from him, and Willis could feel her simmering. He would have to do something to lower her temperature—or raise it. He never minded doing that. Carol was one gorgeous woman. He put his arm around her and pushed back her hair to reveal her ear. He nibbled at the lobe until he felt her start to respond. "I'm sorry, baby," he whispered. "It's just that there's so much riding on this project. I can understand your concern. I don't have to remind you that the whole thing must remain an absolute secret until the work begins. Once ground is broken, Frame Enterprises can't back out."

"That can't happen soon enough for me." She pushed away from him. "Not now, Willis. We need to get a few things straightened out."

Willis sat back and ran his hand through his sandy hair. Carol was getting hard to handle, but handle her he must. "Like what?" he asked as pleasantly as he could.

"Like what happens after they break ground." She had been so busy designing the project that she hadn't been able to think much further ahead than getting the blueprints approved. When they started out together, Willis had promised her a lot of things—money, power, control over her own projects. That was all she had wanted then. She hadn't counted on falling in love with him. Now she still wouldn't mind having the power and the money, but it was Willis she wanted most. And she was going to get him, whether he wanted to be gotten or not.

"What do you mean, what happens after the groundbreaking?" Willis looked at her incredulously. "It'll be the moment I've planned and waited for. With that first shovelful of dirt I shoot right to the top. Socko!" He slammed his fist into the palm of his other hand. "Right between the eyes. Vic and Alice won't know what hit 'em. With the money I make on this project I'll be able to buy up the rest of the stock I'll need to own a controlling interest. I've already started acquiring it. Quietly, of course." Every time he thought about being at the top of Frame Enterprises he felt as if he had grown six inches. Pretty soon he was going to be as big as the Frame office tower itself.

"I see," Carol said coldly. "And what about me? Where do I fit into this picture?"

"Baby, baby," he cooed. "Aren't you standing there right beside me? Isn't your name on those contracts, too? And wasn't I a clever lad to get all that money paid directly to you and me?" He moved toward her and began to run his fingers through her hair. "You're going to be a rich woman, Carol."

"I already am a rich woman." She tossed her head and pulled away from him.

"So you'll be richer." He moved in closer and remounted his assault on her earlobe. He knew she could never resist that for long.

"Sometimes money isn't enough." She felt herself weakening, as she always did when Willis was close to her. She tried to resist, but it was impossible. Her body started to relax; her sharp mind began to blur under the sensation of hot white light that his touch always brought.

Willis continued nibbling and ran his hands up and down her back. "Is anything ever enough?" he whispered.

Carol threw her arms around him and pressed against his hard chest. "You are. You're enough for me."

He laughed as he drew her into a passionate kiss. "I hope so, baby. I certainly hope so."

Chapter Six
Facing Facts

The snow had already been falling for hours when Angie left for work, far earlier than her usual departure time. The last thing she had heard on the radio before going to bed was the weather forecast, and the anticipation of a big snowstorm had wakened her long before the alarm went off. She decided to walk to work and dressed in wool slacks, thick knee socks, and her warmest boots. In a small tote bag she carried a skirt, stockings, and high heels.

Outside, fluffy snow was falling in big flakes that stuck to her cheeks and eyelashes. It was supposed to snow all day and all night and leave Bay City buried under twelve inches or more. Angie loved snow, the quiet and beauty it brought, the way it turned bustling Bay City into a small town. Few people had been out yet, and she forged a path through the unbroken snow, thoroughly enjoying the crunch of the first light layer of white under her boots. The traffic had already slowed, and she heard the rattle of tire chains on many of the passing cars, a modern, dissonant sound, but as natural to her in snow as sleigh bells had been for previous generations.

Her thoughts were devoted to Neal for the first part of the walk. They had had a date last night, as they did most nights lately. They had gone to a basketball game and out for a hamburger afterward. They'd laughed a lot and held hands; Neal had kissed her good-night a number of times. Over the last four weeks she had come to respect him enormously, his humor, his integrity, his enthusiasm. She felt safe with him. Safe, but not excited, not passionate. She enjoyed his kisses, but they didn't set her head spinning, didn't start that whirling feeling in the pit of her stomach.

Only one person did that to her. Try as she might, she couldn't put Willis out of her mind. Or her heart. Neal held a place in her heart, of course, but only in the outer chambers. The secret room still belonged to Willis. She was afraid it would always be that way. Even when she was with Neal, laughing at his jokes, learning about his work, enjoying his embraces, there was always a part of her that was standing outside Willis's door, waiting for him to open it to her. Once, she had fully believed Willis would come back to her, but now he seemed so distant. It was as if that one day in January, when they'd talked about Christmas, had never happened.

Angie arrived at Frame Enterprises well before

most of the other employees. She knew a lot of people would be late today, and some wouldn't make it at all. It was Friday, and if the snow continued as predicted the office was likely to close at lunchtime anyway. But Angie would never miss a day at work on purpose. Coming to work was the only chance she had of seeing Willis, the only chance she had to remind him of what they once had shared.

In the secretary's lounge—an informal room with a sofa and chairs, a table, and a tiny kitchenette—she changed from her wet boots and coat and set the coffee maker going. In minutes the coffee was brewed and she poured a steaming cup into the ceramic mug Neal had given her. It had an angel on the front and a set of wings atop the handle. "Angie Angel," Neal called her. The mug had come with a note: "Come fly with me," it said. How often she had wished she could.

She took a sip of the hot coffee and felt it flow down, beginning to take off the chill of walking in the cold. Neal warmed her in much the same way. Maybe it was just a matter of time before the warmth grew into a spark and set her heart aflame. She hoped so. She couldn't stand living in this kind of limbo for much longer.

She drank half her mug in the lounge, refilled it, and headed for her desk. There was a report for Mr. Blanchard that only needed proofreading. She finished it quickly and went to put it on his desk. As she walked down the hall she saw a

familiar figure coming toward her. Willis was not
a big man, but he walked with an energy and
purpose that made him appear much taller and
broader than he was. Angie's heart skipped a beat
and she tightly clutched the papers she was
carrying.

She smiled nervously as they got closer and
fanned her papers in his direction, but Willis
didn't seem to see her. That's how he was
sometimes, she thought, especially if he was
thinking about something. Willis liked to work
things out in his mind, as if life were a big chess
game and he always had to be three or four moves
ahead.

Just as they were about to pass, Angie smiled
and waved again. Still no response. She couldn't
let him pass her as if she were an absolute
stranger. She found her voice. It was angry.
"Good morning, Willis. Mr. Frame," she added.

The sound of her voice slowed his steps, but he
didn't stop. He looked at her blankly, then said
hello when he had already passed her. He continued down the hall without looking back.

She wanted to shout: "It's me, Angie!" She
wanted to grab his arm and shake him and make
him see her, force him to look at her again as he
once had, back when he had had trouble tearing
his eyes away from her.

But she didn't run after him. She stood rooted
to the carpet, numbed to the bone as she never
had been by cold or wind or rain.

Suddenly an unnatural calm came over her.

She was no longer angry, no longer humiliated. She was empty, completely empty. A shell of Angie was left, a shell she could fill as she chose. She could continue to hope in the face of Willis's indifference, or she could face the facts. She was only one ripple in the constant stream of women who flowed rapidly through Willis's life. Once she had made a small wave, but that was played out now, washed up. She could sit on the shore, lonely and forlorn, or she could slip into the sheltered cove that Neal offered, where it was warm and peaceful.

"Angie, are you all right?" Pam was standing beside her.

Angie snapped out of her reverie. "Sure. Fine," she answered.

"You've been standing here like a statue."

"I was just thinking about something." Suddenly she felt happy and hopeful. "Great weather today, isn't it? I love it when it snows." She smiled at Pam and took off briskly down the hall.

When the official word of early closing came, Angie called Neal immediately. "School's out at noon today. Want to come play with me?"

Neal almost dropped the phone. In all the time they'd been seeing each other, this was the first time Angie had called him to suggest getting together. "That depends on what you want to play," he said suggestively. His pulse was racing even more than usual when he spoke to her. Could she really be coming around to him? He thought he'd sensed her moving closer and closer, but hadn't been sure if it was wishful thinking on his part or not.

"I thought we could build a snowman. I haven't done that in ages."

"Me either. You're on. Meet you in the lobby when we're sprung."

Neal had abandoned the Frame Enterprises formal dress code in light of the weather, and he appeared in the lobby at noon wearing stout boots, corduroys, and a parka. He was surprised and pleased to see Angie similarly dressed. "Don't tell me you braved the executive suite in that outfit," he said as he gave her a hug.

"Of course not. This is what I walked to work in. My real clothes are upstairs in the secretary's lounge."

"You walked to work? In this snow?"

"Very early," she told him. "I had to make the path myself for most of the way."

"You're amazing. Amazingly wonderful." He would have taken her in his arms and kissed her until they were both limp, but there were too many people scurrying past them and out into the storm. He settled for another, bigger hug. "Where do you want to build this snowman?"

"In the park, of course."

They walked to the park, and found the path into it covered with bootprints small and large. Inside the park they heard the shouts and laughter of children, and they followed the sound to a nearby hill. Children in a rainbow of snowsuits were sliding down the hill, some on traditional wooden sleds, some on huge aluminum saucers that glistened in the snow, some on little red plastic disks. Some kids were simply rolling down the hill without the benefit of mechanical conveyance.

Angie and Neal stopped to watch the festivities—the daredevil older children, the tiny ones carefully coached by parents, a few who were more scared than hurt by a tumble. Neal kept his eye on one of the oldest boys, who belly-flopped on his sled after a running start. When he came to the bottom Neal grabbed Angie's hand and hurried over to him before he got very far up the hill. "Hey, kid," Neal called, "want to earn a dollar?"

The boy stopped and looked at them, suspicious but interested. "What do I have to do?"

"Loan me your sled for ten minutes. My friend and I want to take a ride."

Angie's eyes widened. The last thing she could imagine was herself barreling down the hill on a sled. She started to pull on Neal's parka sleeve, but he had already handed the boy a dollar bill and taken the reins of the sled. Warming to the idea, Angie trudged up the hill with him.

It took them a moment to arrange themselves on the sled—it was rather small to accommodate Neal's lanky frame—but finally he was seated with his feet on the steering bar, holding Angie between his knees. He waited for a clear path to open up and then pushed off down the hill. Soon they were rushing down, wind and snow in their faces. Angie started to laugh, then to whoop as they picked up more speed.

"Bonsai!" Neal yelled.

It was impossible for Neal to control the overloaded sled, and they ended up in a heap at the bottom of the hill, a tangle of feet and legs and arms and sled, laughing so hard they could hardly sort themselves out. Their rental agent came to retrieve his property, but Neal reminded him that they still had four minutes on the clock. So they raced up the hill again for a final ride. This time Neal was able to bring the sled to a stop before they ended up in a pile. Reluctantly, they gave the sled back to its owner.

Flushed and panting from their exertions, they walked deeper into the park. "Being with you is like being a kid again," Angie said.

"That's because you bring out the kid in me. When I'm with you, everything is fresh and new, bright and untouched. Like out there." He gestured ahead of them to a field where no one had walked. "Come on." He grabbed her hand and pulled her to the edge of the field. "Let's be the first. Let's make snow angels."

Seconds later they stood with their backs toward the unbroken snow. "All right," Neal said, "on the count of three. One. Two. Three." They both flopped onto their backs with their arms out to the side.

"Now," Angie said, "we have to move our arms up and down, to make the wings."

"Right. I'd almost forgotten that part," Neal said. "But now how do we get up without ruining the impressions?"

They traded ridiculous suggestions until their stomachs hurt from laughter, then decided to sit up and draw their feet in under them, using each other as a balancing post. Several near misses later they had managed to stand without marring the images in the snow. They stepped back and looked at the two perfect angel forms.

Neal held Angie close and impulsively whispered to her, "I love you, Angie Angel. I always want to be this close to you. Marry me."

Angie stared at the snow angels, her mind picturing them with a top hat on one, a lacy veil on the other, like figures on a wedding cake. She'd never been able to imagine it before, marrying Neal, but now she saw the picture very clearly. The wedding, living with him, playing with him. The images flashed before her, colorful, appealing. "Yes," she said before she had time to think anymore. "Yes, I will."

Neal looked at her incredulously. "Did you say yes?"

"Yes," she said again. She reached down and traced the letters in the snow. Y-E-S.

Neal picked her up and whirled her round and round until she was dizzy and begging to be put down. When her head had cleared she noticed that the angels had been damaged. "Oh, no," she cried, pointing at the figures.

"It doesn't matter," Neal said exuberantly.

"We've got the rest of our lives to make angels. And anything else we want."

"I guess you're right," Angie said, but the ruined angels left her with an unsettling feeling.

"Come on," Neal said. "Let's go get some hot chocolate and celebrate."

"Hot chocolate?" Angie asked, trying to retrieve her good humor. "Don't most people celebrate with champagne?"

"Who needs champagne?" Neal planted a kiss on her lips. "I'm as high as I can be right now."

Angie realized she was feeling rather heady, too. "All right," she agreed, "hot chocolate it is. But only if we can have it with the little marshmallows floating in it."

"Why not? We can have whatever we want. We're in love!"

It didn't occur to Neal, not until much later, that Angie had never actually said she loved him.

A cold snap had descended on Chadwell, and the laundry Emma took off the line was cold and stiff. She brought the basket inside and set it in the kitchen. When the clothes warmed up, she would iron and fold them. She heard from the living room the shrieks of contestants on a television game show. Sharlene had done little in the month she had been there except stare at the TV. Emma didn't think she paid any attention to what was on the screen, just kept it on to block out what was on her mind. After all she'd been through, it wasn't surprising that Sharlene didn't want to face life head on, but this funk she was in was going on entirely too long. Emma was getting very worried.

"Sharlene, honey," she called. "Want to help me with these sheets here?"

Sharlene came dutifully into the kitchen. She did whatever Emma asked her to—helped with the cooking, the cleaning, went shopping with her or to the movies—but she was only going through the motions.

As they began folding a sheet, Emma tried to engage her in conversation. "Cold wind's blowing down from the north. Russ Matthews called this morning. He said that Bay City had fifteen inches of snow. Everything's at a halt."

"Russ called this morning and you didn't even tell me?"

"What's the use? You never want to talk to him. Anyway, you were sleeping."

Sharlene shrugged and started to shake out her end of the sheet. She was silent as they folded it into a neat rectangle. Emma reached for another sheet from the basket and handed one end to her sister. "If you want to call Russ," she said, "I'm sure he'd be glad to hear from you."

Sharlene was silent for a long moment. "What would I say?"

"I know what I would say, honey, but I can't put the words in your mouth."

The sisters folded the rest of laundry in silence, putting aside the socks and the things that needed to be ironed. When the basket was empty, Emma got the ironing board from the cupboard and set it up, leaving Sharlene to pair the socks.

"You'd tell him everything, wouldn't you?" Sharlene asked as Emma started on the first shirt.

"That's right. And that's what I think you should do. But I've already said that more than once."

"But you're so strong. You always have been. Not like me."

Emma had never understood Sharlene's lack of self-confidence. She was the only Frame sibling to have an utter lack of faith in herself. Emma hadn't had the success in life that Steve had had, but she had made a decent, comfortable life, a far better one than her parents had been able to give her. And heaven knew that what Willis lacked in sensitivity he made up for in self-confidence. But Sharlene had never been able to cope with life's pain and uncertainty. She had always run away from trouble, but never out of it. She had never learned that facing up to problems could actually help solve them.

"I'm not so strong, Sharlene," she said. "I've never had to pull myself out of the kind of mess that you did. Give yourself credit for being able to leave San Diego behind."

"You'd never have gotten into a situation like that in the first place," Sharlene said, her self-disparagement obvious.

"Maybe, maybe not. If I had, I'm not at all sure I'd have had the courage to get myself back on my feet again." Emma finished the collar of the shirt, hung it up, and reached for another.

Sharlene looked up from her pile of socks. "Really?"

"Really. I didn't just say that to make you feel good."

Despite Sharlene's efforts to make her mind a blank, it had been working those many hours in front of the television. She had tried to imagine how it would be to go back to Bay City, to have Russ's arms around her again, to be able to tell Willis to get out of her life and to stay out. It was easy to picture, but difficult to actually take the first step.

"Russ could never forgive my past. I can't excuse it, so how could I expect him to?" she asked.

"He's a doctor," Emma said. "He understands the weaknesses we all have."

"It wasn't my body that was sick," Sharlene said dully. "It was my mind, my soul."

"I'm sure Russ knows that souls can be cured the same way as bodies."

Sharlene heaved a ball of socks across the room in frustration. "I don't know what to do. I want to go back, really I do, but I can't see myself telling him."

Emma took Sharlene's outburst as a very hopeful sign that she finally had made some inroads with her sister. Maybe if they went back to Bay City and she saw Russ again, she would lose her fear of telling him the truth. "Why don't we take it one step at a time, honey? We'll go back to Bay City. Once you're there, and you know you have me and Alice standing by you, you'll find a way of telling him."

"Maybe," Sharlene said in a small, fearful voice. "I'll try, Emma, honest I will."

Chapter Seven
Under Separate Cover

Pam had been working in Carol's office for over a month, and so far her undercover mission had been a complete bust. There was something going on, she had no doubt about that. Anyone could have figured that out from the locked filing cabinets in Carol's private office and the amount of time she spent talking on her private line, which Pam had been instructed never to answer.

Weeks of vigilance and going through all the open files with a fine-tooth comb had yielded nothing concrete, but today Pam had a solid chance to make her move. The big storm had caused problems at one of the construction sites, and Carol would be out of the office all day. The problems were complex and the construction site was over fifty miles from the office, so there was no chance that Carol would be back before late afternoon. Her added assurance was that Vic had arranged to attend the meeting, too, so he would alert her if it ended earlier than anticipated.

She waited until noon, when the draftsmen and the other assistant had gone to lunch. Then she went into Carol's office and shut and locked the door behind her. The first thing she needed to find was the key to the locked files. She could pry them open with a nail file, but if she did that she might as well leave a note with her signature behind.

Heart beating with nerves and excitement, she went through Carol's desk—a French provincial writing table with one small center drawer. She found Carol's personal stationery, a Mont Blanc fountain pen and a Limoges saucer full of paper clips. She emptied out all the paper clips and sorted through them, but there was no key. Then she removed the drawer from the desk, and felt all around its undersides for a secret compartment or hiding place, but there was nothing. She replaced the drawer and checked beneath the desk and chair, but again found nothing.

There was a small wooden cabinet next to Carol's drafting table, but a thorough search turned up nothing but drafting supplies and a bottle of brandy. Twenty minutes had passed and Pam was starting to worry. The others would be back from lunch soon, and she couldn't risk being seen coming out from behind the locked door of Carol's office. There was nothing suspicious about her being in the office itself, but why would she close and lock the door if Carol weren't there? One of the others might mention it to Carol. One of the others might be watching her every move for Carol. She had no idea how far this spying game had gone, but she couldn't rule out the possibility that Carol and Willis had spies of their own, even if there was nothing concrete to connect her with Vic.

She surveyed the room. Besides the locked file there was a sofa and coffee table, and beyond them the door that led to Carol's private bathroom. *Aha!* Pam thought. The bathroom offered definite possibilities. All those little bottles and jars in the medicine cabinet. She had her hand on the doorknob when the telephone rang. Pam jumped as if the knob were electrified and she'd had a high-voltage shock. After a second, she realized it was Carol's private line ringing. The company phones didn't ring in Carol's private office. She raced to the desk and picked it up before the second ring was complete. "Yes?"

"Ms. Lamonte?" a woman's voice inquired.

"Yes," Pam answered, deepening her voice and blocking her nose as if she had a cold.

"This is Mary Owens in Mr. Jamison's office. He asked me to call to inform you that he and Mr. Pratt will be reviewing the revised blueprints this afternoon, and that he will be calling you in the morning with his opinion."

"Thank you," Pam said, barely able to conceal her glee. The woman said good-bye and Pam put the phone down and hurried back to the bathroom. Jamison & Pratt! They were Bay City's largest real estate developers. She had done no work concerning a project with them since she'd been in Carol's office, so Carol must have some private deal with them. The details had to be locked in that filing cabinet.

Pam almost missed the inside pocket of Carol's zippered case full of expensive cosmetics. The pocket was concealed inside another pocket and had no snap or zipper to announce its presence, but Pam felt a tiny bump and dug inside to find a bonanza. She was more dazzled by the small flat key than she would have been by a large gold nugget.

The key fit the filing cabinet, as Pam suspected it would. The files inside were neat and orderly. She went right to the one labeled JAMISON & PRATT. It was all there: contracts, correspondence, plans. Pam wished fervently for one of those mini-cameras that James Bond carried, the ones shaped like pens or cigarette lighters. Lacking that, she had to rely on her secretarial skills. She'd had the foresight to come into the office with a file folder, in which she'd concealed her stenographic notebook and a sharpened pencil. With lightning speed she copied the contract and correspondence, which Carol apparently had typed herself, after hours, on Pam's typewriter. Pam was more shocked by that than by the under-the-table deal. She smiled as she imagined her elegant boss pecking away at the keys, wondering how she'd managed to turn out the letters without chipping the polish on her long shapely nails.

She replaced the file and the key and checked the room to make sure she had left everything just as she'd found it. She picked up her file, unlocked the door quietly, and re-entered the outer office, as if she had just completed some legitimate errand in Carol's office.

She was so excited she forgot she'd missed lunch. She sat at her typewriter and transcribed her notes, glad that she knew Vic was out of the office. The temptation to call him was overwhelmingly strong. Her fingers flew over the keys as she typed page after page of the purloined documents. When she finished, her neck and back were stiff with tension, her fingers ached from pounding the keys so hard and fast, but she was more proud of that work than any she'd ever done. She locked the typewritten pages and her notebook in the top drawer of her desk and dropped the key securely in her skirt pocket. As she caught up on her afternoon's work she patted it frequently.

The phone call! she thought suddenly in the middle of transcribing a letter. If she didn't leave a message for Carol and the woman from Jamison's office mentioned the call, or if Carol said she hadn't known that Jamison would be calling the following day her goose could be cooked. Better to write out a message on one of the regular pink slips and stick it in the stack with the others, as if it had come in on the regular phone. That could be a problem, because Carol would know the call should have come in over the private line, but Jamison's secretary could have made a mistake. The plan was risky but better than not saying anything at all. She wrote out the slip and put it in among the dozen or so messages she'd already taken.

Carol came into the office about fifteen minutes before Pam would be leaving for the day. Pam handed her the messages and a file full of letters to sign, then began to tidy her desk. Pam was putting the cover on her typewriter when Carol blew out of the office like a tropical storm.

"Did you answer my personal phone, Pam?" The rage in her voice was barely contained.

"Of course not," Pam answered indignantly.

Carol waved a message slip in Pam's face. "This call from Jamison's office came in on the regular line?"

"Yes," Pam said adamantly, marveling at how well she was acting.

"Have you been in my office today?"

"Of course. I put the new cost estimates for the Whitney project on your desk, and that envelope from Mr. Blanchard. Didn't you see them?"

Carol looked at her through narrowed eyes for a long moment, then turned and stalked back into her office, slamming the door behind her. Pam breathed an almost audible sigh of relief and smiled to herself as she slid her chair under her desk.

The first thing Carol did behind the closed door of her office was pour herself a healthy shot of brandy. She drank it down quickly and waited impatiently for its soothing effect to take hold. Then she went to the phone and started to call Bill Jamison's secretary. If she'd told that woman once she'd told her fifty times to never, never call her on the regular company lines. She would have thought Bill Jamison would have smarter, more reliable people in his office.

Before the connection was made, though, she recradled the receiver. This deal was delicate enough. Jamison had already balked at the level of secrecy she and Willis had insisted upon. Chewing out Jamison's secretary would only draw attention to the problem. Tomorrow, as sweetly but firmly as possible, she would remind Mary Owens again to use only her private telephone number.

Pam called Vic at home every ten minutes, bursting at the seams with her news. He didn't get in until almost seven o'clock, and she could hardly contain herself as she told him she had something he absolutely had to see that evening. They arranged to meet at an out-of-the-way diner in one of Bay City's seedier neighborhoods.

"Never say I don't take you to the best places

in town," he said as she slid into the booth opposite him. Pam looked beautiful, even surrounded by flickering fluorescent lights and torn red plastic upholstery. He took her hand across the table. "I've missed you." In the three and a half weeks that Pam had been in Carol's office they'd managed to see each other only once, for dinner in a restaurant twenty miles from Bay City. "When this is over, I'll make it up to you."

"The *Georges Cinq* in Paris couldn't look any better to me tonight," Pam said happily.

"In that case I'll take you here again and save the dough," Vic joked.

"It doesn't look that good," Pam conceded. "I've missed you, too." She squeezed his hand with hers and smiled dreamily at him. Though they'd hardly seen each other, this assignment had made her feel closer to Vic than ever before. Although she was enjoying the work she was doing, she wanted it to be over soon so that they could start seeing each other again. She wanted to know if her feelings had deepened only because of the danger and secrecy, or if not seeing him so much had made her aware of how much he meant to her.

A bored, hard-edged waitress approached and asked if they wanted menus. Vic looked at Pam, who shook her head. "No, thanks," he said to the waitress. "I'll have a cheeseburger deluxe and coffee."

"Same for me," Pam said. The waitress left

without another word and Pam leaned across the table toward Vic. "On my next case, I'm going to make sure I meet my contact in classier places. James Bond wouldn't be caught dead in a place like this."

"You're really getting a kick out of this," Vic said with a laugh.

"It takes some of the boredom out of being a secretary. Hint, hint." Pam raised her eyebrows and smiled.

"Don't worry. I haven't forgotten my promise. In fact, a job has come up that I think you'll be very good for. I just hope we don't have to fill it while I still need you in Carol's office. What's it like working for her?"

"I'm starting to understand the French Revolution," Pam answered wryly. "I can see why they wanted Marie Antoinette's head. What I don't understand is why it took them so long." She reached for the manila envelope with the documents she'd copied. "However, once you see what's in here I have the feeling I won't be in Carol's office too much longer."

She handed the envelope to Vic and sat back. A feeling of intense pleasure suffused her as he ripped open the sealed flap. She didn't like arrogance, greed, or deceit in any form, and she was enjoying having a hand in exposing Carol and Willis's, even if it meant engaging in deceit herself. She had always thought of deceit as merely evil, but now she saw—and felt for herself—the power of it, a tricky and dangerous power that a person could easily get hooked on. She would have to be careful that it didn't happen to her.

"Holy cow!" Vic breathed as he glanced quickly through the papers. "This is unbelievable!"

After the waitress brought their burgers, Pam bit into hers voraciously. She was starving after skipping lunch. But Vic's food went untouched as he examined the papers carefully. By the time he stopped reading, Pam had finished her burger.

He looked dazed as he put the papers back in the envelope. "The audacity of it!" he said and shook his head. "Right under Alice's nose—all our noses. If I hadn't seen the documents I wouldn't have believed it. You realize how serious this is, don't you, Pam?"

She nodded.

"If I were running the company, both of them would be out before they knew what hit them, but Alice will never toss Willis out on his ear. Not unless someone comes up with evidence that he's not really Steve's brother." He grinned at Pam. "You don't think you could come up with something along that line, do you, super-spy?"

"Not unless I made it up myself."

"And you wouldn't stoop that low."

"I've stooped low enough already, Vic. I know it had to be done, but I don't like this business. I was thinking earlier how careful I'll have to be not to get off on a power trip about it."

"You're far too sensible for that."

"I'm also human."

"So I noticed." Vic lowered his voice. "Palpably, touchably human. Right now, no one wants this to be over more than me."

"Except me," she said quietly. The force between them was like two opposing magnets straining to stay away from each other.

"I'm going to do everything possible to wind this up as soon as I can, Pam." He took both of her hands across the table. "Then we can get back together again, where we belong."

"For that, I'd turn in my spy credentials without a second thought."

They didn't notice that the waitress was at their table until she spoke. She was looking down at Vic's untouched plate. "Something wrong with the food?" It was more a challenge than a question.

"No, no," Vic said quickly. "I, uh, wasn't hungry."

She shrugged and gave him a look that said it wasn't any skin off her nose. "More coffee?"

"Please," Vic answered, "and the check."

They held their laughter until the waitress had cleared away the plates. After the waitress returned and refilled their coffee cups, Pam asked, "What are you going to do now, Vic?"

"I honestly don't know. I'd like to sleep on it. There's no sense in calling Alice now. I'll go to

Soaps & Serials™ Fans!

★ Order the *Soaps & Serials*™ books you have missed in this series.

★ Collect other *Soaps & Serials*™ series from their very beginnings.

★ Give *Soaps & Serials*™ series as gifts to other fans.

...see other side for ordering information

You can now order previous titles of *Soaps & Serials*™ Books by Mail!

Just complete the order form, detach, and send together with your check or money order payable to:

Soaps & Serials™
120 Brighton Road, Box 5201, Clifton, NJ 07015-5201

Please circle the book #'s you wish to order:

(A) The Young and The Restless	1 2 3 4 5 6 7 8 9 10 11 12
(B) Days of Our Lives	1 2 3 4 5 6 7 8 9 10 11 12
(C) Guiding Light	1 2 3 4 5 6 7 8 9 10 11 12
(D) Another World	1 2 3 4 5 6 7 8 9 10 11 12
(E) As The World Turns	1 2 3 4 5 6 7 8 9 10 11 12
(F) Dallas™	1 2 3 4 5 6 7 8 9 10 11 12
(G) Knots Landing™	1 2 3 4 5 6 7 8 9 10 11 12

Each book is $2.50 ($3.50 in Canada).
Total number of books circled_____ × price above = $ _____

Sales tax (CT and NY residents only) $ _____

Shipping and Handling $ _____.95

Total payment enclosed $ _____
(check or money orders only)

Name_____

Address _____ Apt#_____

City _____ State _____ Zip _____

Telephone_(_____)_____
AREA CODE

AW 12

her first thing in the morning, when I've had some time to think things through."

"And I'm to carry on as I have been?"

"For the time being, yes. Now that you know what you're looking for it'll be easier to keep your eyes and ears open. But don't take any chances, Pam."

Vic paid the check and they went outside. The streets were still piled with snow from the big storm and there were icy patches on the poorly shoveled sidewalk. He took her arm as they walked to his car. She had taken a taxi to the diner and had wanted to call for one to take her home, but Vic insisted on driving her home himself. "No one's out tonight, and I have to have a few private minutes with you."

Inside the car he took her in his arms and pulled her close. He plucked off her warm wool hat and ran his fingers through her silky hair. "I'm going to kiss you once and then start the car. If I kiss you more they may find us here in the morning, frozen in each other's arms."

Pam smiled and wrapped her mittened hands around his neck. "What a way to go," she whispered.

Every window in the car was fogged by the time Vic lifted his lips from hers. He had to run the defroster for several minutes before he could see well enough to drive.

When they reached her building, Pam hopped out of the car quickly and Vic drove off immediately, taking no more chances than necessary that someone would see them together.

Being apart, however, didn't stop either of them from thinking about the other, deep into the night.

Chapter Eight
Decisions

Vic slept very little that night. When he wasn't wrestling with the problem of what to do about Willis and Carol, he was thinking about Pam. And what he thought about Pam was that he'd like to forget all about his problems and run off to a desert island with her, a place where they could be alone together, where they could make love, talk, swim, walk, do whatever they wanted without the world intruding. But whenever he set up the picture in his mind, Hurricane Willis stormed in to ruin it.

By morning, he had decided the course he would propose to Alice in order to handle Willis. He got up wearily, showered, and dressed in his most somber suit, knowing he would need every device at his disposal to impress Alice with the gravity of the situation. Alice was a smart, rational woman—not as tough as he would have liked her to be where business was concerned, but more than capable of taking charge of Frame Enterprises. Had anyone other than Willis masterminded a plan like this, he was certain Alice would agree that they must be fired. Family loyalty, however, took precedence over everything for Alice. She would never dismiss Willis. But Vic thought he had a plan that would contain the damage Willis had done so far.

Alice was at her desk when Vic arrived at Frame Enterprises. He knocked at the open door of her office and she looked up from her work. He skipped all the preliminaries. "I have something urgent to speak to you about." Without waiting to be invited, he walked into the room and shut the door behind him. The breaches of etiquette were meant to convey the same message as the somber charcoal-gray suit.

Alice was surprised but attentive. "Yes, what is it, Vic?"

Without a word, he handed her the envelope of documents Pam had copied and sat down opposite her desk while she read them.

"What do you recommend we do?" she asked grimly.

"I think you should fire Willis and Carol immediately."

Alice paled, then said in a quiet but firm voice, "You know that's impossible, Vic."

"I know. But I can't be anything less than honest with you, Alice."

"I appreciate that."

"Thank you, but that still leaves us with a very big problem. Frame Enterprises is committed to a major project, and a large percentage of the profits go directly to Willis and Carol. I would like you to issue an executive order, retroactive to the date of the contract, invalidating all contracts you have not personally signed. Then I'll call Bill Jamison, tell him how glad I am that Frame will be building his next luxury apartment complex, and explain—in a friendly way—that because of some internal corporate changes the contracts will have to be drawn up again. His terms will remain exactly the same—the numbers are tight, but I think we can bring it in on budget—but there will be a couple of 'minor' changes on our side of the arrangement. Jamison's got too good a deal to back out, and he must know that he only got it because he's been dealing in secrecy with Willis. He'll make a fool of himself if he doesn't go along with me. Neither you nor I will say anything to Willis. He'll find out from Jamison that we know about the project and, since he won't want to embarrass himself, he'll take his medicine quietly."

Alice was silent for a long time. "How do you come to have these documents?" she asked.

Vic explained how Sharlene's sudden absence had made him suspicious, and told about getting Pam Sloane to replace Sharlene.

There was another long pause. Alice stared thoughtfully out the window while Vic waited patiently for her to come to a decision. "All right," she said finally, "go ahead and call Jamison. I'll write the order immediately and have Angie type it up. Then I'll get her to check the files and pull all the contracts signed during the period. We'll have to bring them all into compliance."

Inwardly Vic felt an enormous sense of relief that Alice had agreed so readily. But the problem of Willis's presence in the company still remained. "Thank you, Alice. I think this will make the best of a bad situation. However, I am concerned that this could happen again, and I must advise you strongly to take whatever measures are necessary to ensure that it doesn't."

"I'll deal with Willis and Carol myself," Alice said resolutely.

"I understand your position," Vic said in a conciliatory tone.

Alice looked at him sadly. "No, I don't think you do," she said, turning her eyes back to the window. She wouldn't elaborate.

When Vic had left the office, Alice rose shakily and shut the door behind him. How would she ever find the wisdom and strength to maintain Frame Enterprises in just the way that Steve would have?

She sat at her desk again and picked up the silver-framed picture of Steve she kept there. Why, why, she asked for the millionth time since the awful telegram arrived, couldn't his body have been found? Living with the certainty of his death would be much easier than harboring the hope that he would somehow, someday reappear. That hope was like a shaft in her heart that prevented it from healing. The wound was as raw today as it had been the day she got the news.

The faint hope that Steve was not dead made it imperative that she maintain Frame Enterprises. When—if—Steve returned, he must find the company he had worked so hard to found and build intact. But, because of Willis, she was in danger of losing control over the company.

Willis would never be able to run the company the way Steve had. Willis did not have his vision, his fair-mindedness, his humanity. Willis had many good qualities—energy, enthusiasm, drive, tremendous powers of concentration—but they were qualities that he used only in the service of himself. He would never be able to see the larger picture, as Steve had. With Willis at the head of the company, the strong, free-flowing river Steve had created would branch off into hundreds of weak, meandering streams.

Yet Willis was Steve's brother. He was family. She couldn't toss him out, as Vic had advised, nor could she confront him directly. She knew him well enough to know that that would only make him more determined to get the better of her. She would have to find a way to harness Willis's abilities. But first she had to deal with the problem at hand.

She called Angie into her office and dictated the order requiring her signature on all Frame Enterprises contracts. Not until Angie was seated opposite her desk did Alice realize she should have called one of the other executive secretaries. Angie might mention the order to Willis before Vic had completed his talk with Jamison. But then it occurred to her that Angie had no way of knowing why she was dictating the order, and so she would not go to Willis, despite her past relationship with him. As she began to dictate, it struck Alice how ill-suited she was for this kind of devious, convoluted thinking.

She watched Angie's hands as she took down the order and suddenly noticed that there was a small diamond ring on Angie's left hand. When she finished dictating she asked, "I hope you won't think I'm nosy, but is that an engagement ring you're wearing?"

"Yes, it is." Angie wriggled the fingers of her left hand. Although the diamond Neal had given her was small, she felt the weight of it all the time.

"Congratulations," Alice said. "Who's the lucky man?"

"Neal Johnson."

"Oh, yes, the young architect. I've heard very good things about him from Mr. Delaney. I hope you'll be very happy." Alice spoke warmly, for she knew of Angie's experience with Willis. She was glad Angie had gotten over it and found happiness with another man.

"Thank you, Mrs. Frame," Angie said softly. She felt odd talking to Willis's sister-in-law about her engagement. After all, Alice knew about her past involvement with Willis and must have had strong feelings about it, even though she seemed quite sincere in her good wishes. "Will there be anything else?"

Alice issued instructions to search the files for contracts that were not in compliance with the new order. She thanked Angie and waited until she left the room. Then Alice sat back in her chair, feeling marginally more hopeful. Seeing Angie had given her an idea.

While Willis was with them, the women in his life had a great deal of influence over him. He probably wouldn't agree with her about that, but she had noticed that he was never long without steady female companionship. He needed a woman by his side. Right now that woman was Carol Lamonte. Alice and Carol had never gotten along particularly well, but they were both women, and the men they loved were brothers. That was enough of a connection for Alice to feel comfortable approaching Carol. She would talk to her, woman to woman, in hopes of reaching Willis.

Feeling decidedly better now that she had hit upon a course of action, Alice buzzed Angie and asked her to have Mr. Hastings come to her office as soon as possible.

Vic, too, was feeling better, and had good news for Alice once he was settled in her office. "I just got off the phone with Bill Jamison. The plan worked like a charm. He blustered a bit when I first mentioned rewriting the contract, but as soon as he heard his terms would remain the same, he was like putty in my hand. He had suspected Willis was being a bit precipitate, but no real estate developer in his right mind could turn down the deal Willis was offering. In the long run, Alice, this may turn out very well. We've been trying to get Jamison and Pratt's business for a long time now."

Alice felt herself relax for the first time since Vic had walked into her office that morning. "And I've figured out what to do about Willis," she told him.

"That was quick," Vic said jauntily. Maybe Alice had come to her senses and decided to fire Willis and Carol.

"Carol is the key to Willis. She'll be able to tell me what to do to get Willis to work with us, not against us, the same way you turned around this Jamison and Pratt deal."

Vic stared at Alice in disbelief. "But Willis and Carol are in this thing together, thick as thieves. If you go to her, you'll be playing right into Willis's hands."

"I don't think so." Point by point she explained the thinking that had led her to that conclusion.

As he listened, Vic realized that Alice's plan was not as crazy as it had seemed on first hearing; still, he was not at all convinced it would work. "I can see you're determined, Alice, no matter what I say. I hope you're right. But you'll have to wait until tomorrow to find out. I had to send

Carol back out to Somerset this morning." He winked conspiratorially. "I found a few more things that needed her personal attention."

"It's Friday. That means I won't be able to talk to her until Monday." Alice sighed. "You know I don't like these corporate games, Vic."

"Time, Alice," he counseled. "We're buying time. It's the only thing we have on our side. Monday will be time enough for Carol. She and Willis will be well on the defensive by then."

She would never understand all the strategy and one-upmanship, Alice thought bleakly after Vic left. But the best she could do was make her own plays according to her own rules. She picked up the phone and left a message that Carol was to come to her office first thing Monday morning.

Emma patted Sharlene's hand reassuringly as their taxi left the Bay City airport. "Everything's going to be fine, honey; you just relax now." Sharlene didn't say anything, so Emma kept up a stream of inconsequential chatter. "I always did like Bay City. It seems so clean and cozy, especially under this snow. It certainly will be nice to have a good long visit with Alice. And that house is something else! To think a brother of ours could have built a mansion like that."

"It is a beautiful house," Sharlene agreed quietly. "There's so much of Steve in it, I sometimes feel he's there." Emma had been right. Going back was not going to be nearly as bad as she had imagined. She was nervous, but with

Emma and Alice for support she somehow would be able to get her life back on track, explain to Russ, deal with Willis.

Mrs. Marsh greeted them at the door with the news that Alice would be a little late getting home from the office. She showed Emma to her room, right next door to the one Sharlene had been using, and offered a cup of tea in the family room as soon as they had freshened up. Sally joined her aunts after they had unpacked, and the three were in the family room when Alice arrived.

"Emma! Sharlene! How wonderful to have you both here with me," Alice exclaimed. The women exchanged hugs, and Alice greeted her daughter with a kiss. The excited chatter continued through Mrs. Marsh's dinner, Emma doing the lion's share of the talking, Sharlene doing the least. Exhausted by nerves and anticipation, Sharlene went up to bed soon after Sally had been tucked in.

Emma and Alice refilled their coffee cups and settled down in front of the fire together. "Tell me about Sharlene," Alice said. "I don't really understand why she ran off so suddenly. She seemed to be doing so well here with me."

"Sharlene's never been much good at sticking through the tough times. She got scared and ran off. It's not the first time."

"But scared of what?"

Emma's natural honesty impelled her to tell Alice everything—about Sharlene in San Diego, about Willis's threats—but she had promised not to tell anyone. "About getting married again," she answered. It wasn't the whole truth, but it was a goodly part.

"Getting married! To whom?"

Emma was stunned. "To your brother. I assumed you knew."

Alice put her cup on the coffee table, not trusting herself to hold it without spilling the contents. "No, I didn't know. But it's starting to make sense. I've had the feeling Russ was keeping something from me lately, but I hadn't a clue what it was. I didn't want to seem like I was prying, so I never asked—" Alice broke off and started to laugh. "You know, Russ was here the night Sharlene disappeared. He seemed too interested for someone who'd only casually gone out with Sharlene a few times, but I was so worried about her that Russ's concern didn't really register with me."

By now Emma was laughing, too. "I assumed it was you who gave him my phone number, even though Sharlene said he must have snooped around to find it."

"Sharlene must be right," Alice concluded. "I promised her I wouldn't give out the number. He probably overheard my conversation and copied it off the hall pad somehow. Has he been calling?"

"Several times a day. Sharlene finally came to the phone a few days ago."

"So he knows she's back."

"No, she wouldn't tell him and insisted I not tell him, either. That's Sharlene for you. To look at her, you'd think a strong wind would snap her in two, but she's tough. Not as tough as this old bird, though." She gave Alice a conspiratorial grin. "What are we going to do about it?"

"Well . . . we could have a special dinner for you and Sharlene. And I could invite my brother. As well as the rest of my family and a few other friends. It's not against the law to invite your own brother to dinner, is it?"

"Certainly not," Emma agreed emphatically.

For a moment Alice was very pleased with herself and her plan; then her face turned serious. Emma asked if anything was wrong.

"Not wrong, exactly. I made a very self-righteous comment today at work about not liking corporate games, and here I am playing my own games, making clever moves I would never approve of at the office."

"Does that mean you're not going to invite him?"

"Oh, I'll invite him, all right. Where the happiness of my family is concerned, I have few scruples. And Steve's family is my family."

"So you're under the double whammy." As both women chuckled philosophically, an uncomfortable thought occurred to Emma. "Are you planning to invite Willis to this shindig?"

Alice hadn't considered Willis. Under the circumstances, she would find it hard to entertain him in her home, but she didn't want to offend

Emma. "There's a rather unpleasant situation at the company just now, Emma, so—"

Emma held up her hand. "I understand. We're used to 'unpleasant situations' with Willis. I think I'll phone my little brother tomorrow, let him know I'm in town." That should head him off at the pass, for a while at least, Emma thought.

The party was hastily planned for Sunday evening. By six forty-five, Mrs. Marsh was putting the finishing touches on the evening meal. Following cocktails and hors d'oeuvres, the twelve guests would dine on cream of spinach soup, roast beef with Yorkshire pudding, and lemon tart. The table in the formal dining room had been set with the Wedgwood dinner service and the Waterford crystal; the furniture in the living room had been polished to a high gloss.

Upstairs, Alice dressed in a pale blue silk sheath, a classic dress with scoop neckline and long fitted sleeves. Steve had had it made for her on a business trip to the Far East. She would always wear it, and always with the pearls that she had found nestled in the box with the dress. There was a catch in her throat as she fastened the pearls around her neck. Steve had always done that for her, had always been with her to greet their guests. Tonight—and every night —she would have to do it all alone.

Down the hall, Emma muttered an oath as she struggled with the zipper on her serviceable black wool. Since the last time she'd had occasion to wear the dress, she'd put on a few pounds. She would have to be careful not to add to them while she was there, although with Mrs. Marsh's home-made Danish pastry, she didn't know how that would be possible. She also didn't know how it would be possible to fend off Willis until Sharlene had told Russ the truth. There was so much about the situation she had no way to control.

There was a knock at the door, and Sharlene stuck her head in. "Come in, honey," Emma said. "Let me see your dress."

Sharlene walked into the center of the room and turned around slowly. The lemon-yellow two-piece knit was a lovely contrast to Sharlene's dark hair and eyes. Sharlene herself looked more rested and peaceful than she had in weeks. "You look beautiful," Emma complimented her.

"Since Russ is coming tonight, I made a special effort."

Emma felt a guilty blush spread over her face. "Alice and I weren't sure how you'd take it, so we didn't tell you."

"I wasn't absolutely certain he'd been invited, but then how could Alice throw a dinner party and not invite her brother? I wish you had let me know instead of leaving me to wonder. How do you expect me to grow up if you keep treating me like a little kid?"

"You're absolutely right, honey. I apologize. But I'm glad you've seen how it feels to have the shoe on the other foot. About telling people things, I mean."

"Don't lecture me," Sharlene said sharply, immediately regretting her words. "I'm sorry," she apologized. "It's just that I'm nervous."

"I understand, but do think about what I said."

"It's all I ever think about. I wish I could stop thinking about it."

"That's entirely up to you." The chime of the doorbell floated upstairs. "That must mean it's time for us to go downstairs." Emma put an arm around her sister's shoulder and squeezed her comfortingly.

Alice, Sharlene, and Emma met in the hall and went downstairs together. They stationed themselves at the door to the living room to receive the guests. Russ was the last to arrive. "Sorry," he said to Alice as he kissed her cheek. "I couldn't get away from the hospital."

Alice could tell that he was nervous. She turned toward Emma to make the introduction, but Russ had already moved on.

"You must be Emma," he said, offering his hand. She looked exactly the way he'd imagined her—solid, handsome, and practical. She shook his hand heartily.

"Very pleased to meet you. I believe you know my sister, Sharlene," she said dryly.

Russ grinned despite his nervousness and turned to Sharlene. She had her head averted, but she turned toward him when he said her name. "Hello, Russ," she said timidly.

Alice touched Russ lightly on the shoulder. "The morning room is empty," she said. "Take as much time as you need. I'll hold dinner." She nudged Emma, and the two women moved into the room to mingle with the rest of the guests.

"I guess the cat's out of the bag," Russ said to Sharlene after an awkward moment.

"When you kept calling Chadwell, I had to tell Emma, and she told Alice— I'm not sure if there's anything to tell anymore, Russ."

"Yes, there is." He guided her across the hall and into the morning room, a small study furnished in soft, spring-inspired floral fabrics. "There's this to tell." He took her into his arms and pressed his lips fervently to hers. "I love you. I am happy and grateful and relieved that you're back." He kissed her again, crushing her slender body to his. "I was so afraid I'd never get to hold you again."

Sharlene clung to him, allowing herself to feel how much she had missed him, how much she needed and loved him. "I'm sorry I ran off the way I did."

"So am I," he whispered. "You almost drove me crazy. I kept imagining the rest of my life without you. It was so bleak, so endless."

"Oh, Russ." She choked back a sob. "I didn't mean to hurt you. I'll never do anything to hurt you again. I promise."

He took her face between his hands and looked

deep into her eyes. "Just don't go away. As long as you're here I can deal with anything. No, *we*," he amended, "can deal with anything if we're together."

Wrapped in the warmth and security of Russ's arms, Sharlene felt the truth of his words. As long as they were together they could face anything, including Willis. "We have to talk, Russ. There's something I have to tell you."

He put a finger over her lips. "Not now, darling. I just want to hold you for a few minutes. Later you can tell me anything you want. We'll have the rest of our lives for you to spin out your story."

Sharlene leaned against him, suddenly weary, as if she had run a very long race. It was over, and she had lost. The moment had passed when she could have blurted out everything, told him about every black mark on her soul. She wasn't sure another moment would ever arise, or that she would have the strength to take advantage of it if it did. She held on to him tightly, telling herself that it didn't matter. All that mattered was that they were together.

"I'd like you to do something for me." Russ took a step back from her and took both her hands in his. "I'd like you to allow me to announce our engagement tonight. In the dining room, before dinner."

Sharlene's stomach tightened automatically, but then she looked into Russ's eyes, shining with love for her, a love she returned from the bottom of her heart. She could refuse him nothing, not after he'd taken her back unconditionally and without reproach. "I'm ready," she said simply.

He clasped her close again. "Oh, Sharlene," he murmured. "I love you so much."

"And I love you, Russ. I promise I'll do everything I can to be worthy of your love."

"I know that, darling." He tipped his head to kiss her again. "What are we waiting for?" he asked eagerly when he released her. "Let's go tell Alice and the others." He grinned at her boyishly. "If I know my sister, she's got champagne on ice. Just in case. Wanna bet?"

"Sure. Ten kisses says she doesn't."

"And twenty says she does."

Russ won the bet, but neither of them counted the kisses at the payoff.

Chapter Nine
Power Play

Carol was not looking forward to meeting with Alice first thing Monday morning. She was sure Alice had learned about the Jamison & Pratt deal, and she'd give her eyeteeth to know how she had found out. Carol certainly hadn't told anyone, nor had Willis; neither of their offices had been disturbed. Somewhere along the line word had leaked out, though. She'd had to employ a freelance draftsman to work on the plans, and she had no control over the people in Jamison's office. Maybe one of them was in some way connected with Frame Enterprises. No matter what happened in Alice's office now, she was determined to find out how the leak had occurred. Not that she was totally disappointed that the deal was out in the open. Keeping something that big a secret was too hard a job, especially with all the other work the project entailed. She and Willis seemed to talk of nothing else lately.

The session with Alice would undoubtedly be unpleasant. Carol wasn't afraid of being fired. She was too deeply involved with too many Frame projects. It would cost the company a lot of money to get rid of her. But if Alice did fire her, she knew she could find another job without any trouble. She knew how good she was. She might even look for financial backing and set up her own shop, as she'd often thought of doing.

What bothered her was Alice. Carol thought of herself as a self-assured, confident woman, yet when she was in the same room with Alice she felt unsure of herself, even meek. No one else she had ever met provoked that kind of response in her. She didn't like it, and she didn't understand it. It wasn't as if Alice were an imposing type, either in disposition or in achievement.

Carol was determined not to let Alice get the better of her this morning. She strode into the office after a perfunctory knock. "You wanted to see me, Alice?"

Alice ignored Carol's aggressive tone. "Good morning," she replied pleasantly. She was determined to get Carol off the defensive immediately. That was the only way she could get her to open up. "Make yourself comfortable, please." She offered coffee and sweet rolls from the tray she'd had sent up, but Carol refused. "Help yourself if you change your mind," she said, pouring a cup of coffee for herself.

Carol was thrown off-balance by Alice's gracious-hostess act, and annoyed at herself for being so thrown. "I don't think you invited me here for breakfast."

"No, I didn't. But I didn't invite you here for a confrontation either." Alice stirred her coffee and broke off a piece of sweet roll. "First I want to say that I'm very disappointed that you let yourself be swept along with Willis's plans for this project with Jamison and Pratt. It was disloyal and self-serving."

That was it, Carol realized. She made her feel like a prep-school student being chastised by the headmistress.

"I've been advised to terminate your services," Alice continued, "but I don't want to do that. First, because you are a talented and valuable employee, and second, because I need your help."

Carol was not quick enough to hide her surprise. "What could you possibly need my help with?"

"Willis."

Carol looked at Alice cannily. Maybe Alice wasn't as naïve as she seemed. "What about Willis?"

"I have an obligation to my husband to ensure that Frame Enterprises is run the way he would have run it. Willis seems determined to prevent me from doing that. I believe you genuinely care about Willis, Carol. I want to know why you think he needs to undermine me, and what I can do to stop him from continuing on his course."

"Why don't you ask Willis what he wants?"

"Because I don't think he'd be honest with me."

"And you think I will?"

"I'm appealing to you woman to woman, Carol. Not as the head of Frame Enterprises, but because I have two conflicting obligations—to my husband's business and to the well-being of his family."

Carol thought for a moment. If she were in Alice's shoes she'd have sent Willis and herself packing. But here was Alice, offering not a rout, not even a tie, but a brand-new game. Only a fool would turn that down. "I don't believe in all this sentimental claptrap, Alice, but I'm going to be straight with you, because I think it's to all of our advantage. Give Willis complete and unquestioned responsibility for some area of the company. He needs something to call his own; he can't be Steve Frame's little brother for the rest of his life, especially now that Steve's"—she started to say "dead," but sought a more delicate word, a concession that no one but Alice could have wrung from her—"um, not around. If he doesn't have to spend so much time proving himself, most of all to himself, he'll settle down and be a shrewd, creative manager."

"I can see what Willis and I get out of such a plan," Alice answered, "but I don't see any advantages for you. What do you get?"

"I get more of Willis's time."

Alice smiled for the first time during the

meeting. So there *was* a heart beneath Carol's cool, competent exterior. "Yes, time with the man you love is the most important thing you can have." It was a lesson she'd learned too late, too painfully.

"Is there anything else?" Carol started to get up.

"No, thank you. I'll think carefully about what you've said."

Carol nodded and left Alice's office swiftly. She had a lot to talk over with Willis.

Alice finished her coffee and roll slowly, thinking about what Carol had said. When she came to a decision, she walked down the hall to Vic's office.

"How did it go with Carol?" he asked.

"Very well," Alice said. She recounted her conversation with Carol and began to explain her plan to Vic. "I know you're not going to like this, but I hope I can count on your loyalty to help me see it through."

"When you start talking about loyalty, I smell trouble," Vic said lightly, "but let 'er rip, Alice."

"I would like to give Willis responsibility for the acquisition and development of new projects. He'll come up with the ideas, court the people, put together the deals. He'll come to me only when he needs my signature on a contract. Once a contract is signed, the project comes under your total and complete control. Willis goes on to the next project. Which means that you are now responsible for Jamison and Pratt."

Vic had a dozen objections he could think of off the top of his head, but he voiced none of them. He wanted to get Alice to see the folly of her plan herself. "I believe you know that I can be trusted to abide by the rules you lay down, Alice, but I'm not sure you'll get that kind of cooperation from Willis—based on his past record, of course. What happens when he refuses to relinquish control over a project?"

"Then I am prepared to turn Willis out," she said shakily. "He can keep the stock that Steve settled on him. He can vote at shareholders' meetings, just like any other stockholder. But he will have no voice in the day-to-day running of the company."

Vic looked at Alice with admiration. "You *have* heard some of what I've said, haven't you?"

Alice responded to his compliment with a pained smile. "This isn't going to be easy for me. I need your support if I'm to carry out this plan."

"You were right when you said I wouldn't like this. I don't, but if you're prepared to fire Willis if he oversteps his bounds again, then I'm willing to give it a chance. I must warn you, however, that if Willis doesn't comply, and you aren't able to fire him, I will have to withdraw my services from Frame Enterprises. Reluctantly, of course."

"I understand, Vic."

Willis awaited the summons to Alice's office eagerly. Carol had just left his office after telling him the good news. Alice had to be the world's most gullible woman. Instead of wanting his head *on* a silver platter, she wanted to present him *with* a silver platter. He imagined with glee the scene in which he would humbly and gratefully accept her offer. He might even apologize. Yes, he would apologize. Alice would like that. He hadn't traded on her rigid old-fashioned morality nearly enough, but now he would be sure to use it to his advantage.

When the call came, his impulse was to keep Alice waiting, but then he decided against it. Better to appear chastened, a bit anxious, eager to please. He rumpled his hair slightly, loosened the knot on his tie a tad. He even slumped his shoulders when he walked into Alice's office.

He kept his shoulders slumped as Alice expressed her disappointment in him for his betrayal of Steve's trust. When she offered him responsibility for all new development for the company, he practically groveled at her feet. Then he apologized and promised that he would never do anything dishonorable again.

"I sincerely hope you won't," Alice told him.

Willis was prepared to leave the office then, but Alice kept talking. As she spoke, his shoulders straightened perceptibly.

"I'm sorry to have to say this, Willis," Alice was saying, "but in light of past performance, I'm afraid I have to ensure in some way that you won't continue to undermine me."

So that was the game, Willis thought, as Alice outlined her terms: one slip and he was out.

Well, we'll see about that, Alice Blue Gown. We'll just see. He made himself slump in his chair again, even let his head hang dejectedly.

"It won't come to that, Alice. Honestly. I care too much about Frame Enterprises to do anything that would mean I'd have to leave it. I appreciate your lenience, and I'll do my best to bring credit to the company. In fact, I have an idea for what could turn out to be the most prestigious project the company's ever been involved in."

Willis snowed Alice for five minutes or so with talk of an Olympic sports complex that would serve as a central training area for all American world-class athletes. He'd tossed the idea around with a Bay City Council member a few weeks before. Nothing would ever come of it, but it sounded good—patriotism, uplifting the youth of the land, all the jive that Alice and dear departed Steve sopped up and lived off, like gravy on bread. By the time he'd finished he had himself believing in the project. Maybe he'd take that councilman to lunch this week.

He left Alice's office feeling energetic and optimistic. That phone call from Bill Jamison on Friday had been an ill wind, but it appeared to be blowing good his way, after all.

Vic worked with the legal department well into the night to prepare the new Jamison & Pratt contracts. When he sent them out, he had Bill Jamison's assurance that he would have them back by the end of the week. But on Friday morning they had not arrived. Vic called Jamison and got the runaround, which made him both angry and suspicious. Jamison had a reputation as a straight shooter. Could Jamison or his company be in financial trouble? That was something Willis should have researched before doing business with them. Vic decided he'd better find out everything he could about what was going on at Jamison & Pratt and with the principals of the company. He also called Pam and asked her to find out if Carol or Willis had anything to do with the delay on the contracts.

At lunchtime, Pam went to Willis's office with a file full of reports Carol had asked her to prepare for him. Earlier she had overheard him bragging to Carol about a lunch date at a fancy French restaurant with a Bay City Council member, so she knew he would be gone for at least two hours. She made sure no one had seen her enter the office, then shut and locked the door behind herself.

Her stomach rumbled loudly as she started to search through the papers on Willis's desk. If she stayed on this assignment much longer, she was going to need intravenous feeding to make up for all the missed lunches. She hoped it wouldn't take her long to find something useful, and she hoped that this would be the last time her services were needed. She was tired of the game and wanted to get back to a real life.

She discovered quickly that Willis was not as fastidious as Carol about secrets. Every drawer in his desk was open. Inside the center one, along with a hodgepodge of pens, pencils, paperclips, and paper scraps, she found an overstuffed file marked "J & P." She pulled it out and began to go through it. Within minutes she found a letter so inflammatory it nearly burned her fingers. She also found a penciled note: "$ to BJ: Feb 21. 10M." She let out a soft whistle.

Mission accomplished, with time to spare for lunch. Except that she wasn't hungry anymore. She copied the letter in shorthand, put the original back in the file along with the note, and replaced the file in the drawer, careful to leave the contents in the same disarray in which she'd found them. She let herself out of the office, booty concealed in her file folder, and raced to her desk to type out the letter.

The executive suite was still in its lunchtime lull when she went to Vic's office to make her report. She was just about to knock on the door of his office when it opened and Angie came out.

"Pam! Excuse me," Angie said, startled. "I didn't expect to see anyone outside the door. How're things going in the architecture department?"

Pam recovered and smiled brightly at Angie.

"Just fine, thanks. Is Mr. Hastings in? I have some papers for him."

Vic called from his desk. "Come right in—Ms. Sloane, isn't it? What brings you to this neck of the woods?"

"Ms. Lamonte asked me to bring these to you." She went into the room and started to close the door behind her, but Vic motioned to her to leave it open, subtly cocking his head in Angie's direction as explanation. Pam came into the room and offered Vic the file folder. "She asked me to wait for a reply."

"Have a seat, please."

Angie had started back to her desk, but when she heard Vic say, "Ms. Sloane, isn't it?" something clicked in her mind. Pam had been out of the department for just over a month. Vic wouldn't have forgotten her name in that short a time. She hung back, out of sight behind the open door. She couldn't hear every word Pam and Vic said, but she could piece together the conversation well enough.

"You found this letter in Willis's desk?" Vic asked Pam very quietly.

"It wasn't even locked up. Has the smoke stopped coming out of my ears?" Pam asked. "The audacity of it is astounding."

Vic read a couple of sentences of the letter addressed to him. "You're telling me! 'Until such time as the renegotiated contracts are countersigned by an officer of Jamison & Pratt, Inc., I consider myself in full charge, per Alice Frame's recent order, of the luxury apartment building under development. Although it is not required of me, I will supply you, at my convenience, with copies of all correspondence regarding this project, until such time as the project is no longer under development.' At his convenience! The contracts will conveniently not be signed, so the project will officially be under development until it's finished."

"Do you think the '10M to BJ' ensures an indefinite delay with the contracts?" Pam asked. They were speaking in whispers, but she still felt uncomfortable about that open door.

"It's hard not to think that," Vic replied.

Angie had heard all she needed—or wanted—to hear. She didn't know who Jamison & Pratt were, but this letter Willis had written probably meant big trouble for him. It had to mean big trouble if Pam had taken the risk of stealing it from his desk. She didn't know why Pam should be going through Willis's desk, but it couldn't be good for Willis. She went right to Willis's office to tell him. He wasn't there, but she left a note on his desk, telling him she had to see him as soon as he came back.

Vic, unaware of Angie's actions, sat back in his chair and read the letter again, debating what to do. He decided to do nothing for the time being. He would give Willis enough rope to hang himself. Then he'd go to Alice. She'd have no choice but to get rid of him then. He would, however, have to do something to shield Pam. "This is all getting too hot. I want you out of Carol's office. Today. You can tell her this will be your last day. You've been offered a transfer to be assistant manager of the construction supply department, and you've accepted."

"I have?" Pam asked with a happy grin.

"Enjoy your weekend," Vic advised, "because starting Monday morning you are going to work your butt off."

"Does this mean I'm going to have someone to enjoy the weekend with?"

"Sure. I'll make a reservation at the diner."

"The heck you will," Pam shot back. "Make it that little French place on Anderson. The very expensive one. I've always wanted to go there."

Angie went to Willis's office every ten minutes to see if he was there. Finally, she found him at his desk. "Didn't you get my note?"

"I got it," he answered curtly. He had been too preoccupied lately to carry through on the peace-making effort he'd begun with her weeks ago. He certainly couldn't be bothered with that today. It wasn't that important, not with everything else he had to worry about. "What is it now, Angie? I thought it was all settled between us. Aren't you going to marry that Johnson guy?"

"This has nothing to do with Neal," she said stiffly. Why was she here? Why did she still care about Willis? Why did she let him treat her this way? She should walk out on him, let him suffer the consequences.

"Then what does it have to do with?"

"I overheard something that might be of interest to you," she said coolly. This was the last thing she would ever do for him. After this she'd never think about him, never talk to him unless it was absolutely necessary. "I think I'd better shut the door."

Willis waited impatiently. He never cared for the way she had to turn every little thing into a major dramatic event. However, she did have the run of the executive suite and could indeed have some genuinely useful information. It couldn't hurt to turn on a little charm. "Now, tell me what you've heard with those gorgeous little ears."

Willis couldn't believe his luck when he heard what Angie had to say.

"Angie, baby, you are a doll, an absolute living doll. You may not know it, but you have saved my life." He got out of his chair and swept her into his arms. "I'll always be grateful for this. Always." He pulled her close and kissed her soundly. She struggled a little at first, but he didn't let her go.

"I wish you hadn't done that, Willis," Angie said shakily when he finally let her go.

"So do I," he cooed. "I'd almost forgotten how sweet and beautiful you are." He kissed her again. "Almost but not quite."

Angie wanted to lean against him, wrap her arms around him, never let him go, but she forced herself to pull away, forced herself to think of all the times Willis had hurt her. Without another word she fled from the room.

Willis wiped away Angie's lipstick with his handkerchief, wondering why she was marrying the Johnson guy when it was apparent she was still in love with him.

After leaving Vic's office, Pam had a leisurely lunch in the cafeteria and ambled back to her desk. "Where've you been?" Carol snapped when she saw Pam enter the office.

"Could I have a word with you, please?" Pam asked sweetly.

"The revisions for Somerset have to get out this afternoon, Pam. Neither of us has time for a chat."

"The revisions are finished, and I do have something very important to say to you."

"All right," Carol relented, "but please make it quick." Although she couldn't fault Pam's work, she had never really liked the woman. She liked more submissiveness and deference from a secretary.

With unconcealed relish, Pam told Carol about her promotion.

"How very nice for you," Carol said, not bothering to try for enthusiasm.

Pam gave her an exaggerated thank-you and

turned to go. "I'll bring those revisions in right away." On her way out the door, she ran smack into Willis.

He glowered at her for a moment and then said in a low, menacing voice, "You're fired."

"No," she said evenly. "I'm promoted. I'll be assistant manager in construction supply on Monday morning."

Willis was flabbergasted. "We'll see about that." He stalked into Carol's office and slammed the door.

"What was that all about?" Carol asked. Willis told her, and she sank wearily onto the sofa. It had been a long week, a very long week. "Now what are we going to do?"

"I'm going to have to find another way to keep the Jamison and Pratt project under my control."

"And enough money to do it. You'll bankrupt yourself, Willis."

"I don't care. It's my project and I'll be damned if I'm going to let Alice Blue Gown and Sir Galahad Hastings take it away from me."

Carol pushed herself off the couch and got the brandy bottle out of the cabinet beside her drafting table. The week had taken its toll; the bottle was nearly empty, but there was enough for two small glasses. She handed one to Willis. "Why don't you give it a rest? So what if Alice and Vic chalk one up on their side of the scoreboard. Concentrate on developing a fabulous new project, a dozen new projects. Work on the Olympic sports complex. Think what a feather in your cap that would be."

"I want to keep the feather I already have."

"Even if you lose the head that wears the cap," she said sourly. "You're acting like an adolescent, Willis."

"Am I? You seemed to think I was a grown-up man last night."

"What happened last night has nothing to do with this."

"Yes, it does. You're either with me or against me, baby. Take your pick."

After a long pause, Carol answered wearily. "I'm with you." She didn't have the stamina to argue with Willis then, but she would soon. All she needed was a little time to recoup.

Chapter Ten
The Pawn in the Game

"You've been a million miles away all weekend, Angie," Neal remarked on Sunday afternoon. They'd taken a walk in the park after lunch and had come back to Angie's apartment. The whole afternoon he had felt as if he were an adolescent trying to make conversation with a painfully shy blind date. Nothing he said seemed to penetrate the invisible wall around her.

"Have I?" She wasn't aware of being particularly quiet; but then, since Friday afternoon in Willis's office she hadn't been aware of much. She was still shaken by Willis's kiss and had thought of little else. "More hot chocolate? There's still some left in the pan."

"No. All I want is to know what's the matter with you. Has something happened that you're not telling me about?"

I ought to tell him, Angie thought. But he was so

134

sensitive about Willis. "No," she said, pasting a bright smile on her face. "I'm just a little tired, that's all. I'm sorry if I haven't been very good company. Can I make it up by letting you beat me at gin rummy?"

"Good offer," Neal said with a chuckle, "but not good enough. Come here—" he held out his arms "—and let me hold you."

Angie moved over on the couch into his embrace. He lifted her face for a kiss. "I love you, Angie," he said before dropping his lips tenderly on hers.

She tried to relax and respond to his kiss, but even the warmth and security she usually felt in Neal's arms wasn't there anymore. The more she tried to recapture the feeling, the more elusive it became.

Neal pulled away from her and turned away. "Have I done something? Are you angry with me for some reason? I feel like I'm kissing a rag doll." A thought suddenly struck Neal full force. "You don't want to marry me. That's it, and you don't know how to tell me."

"No, no," Angie said quickly. "I want to marry you. I want us to be happy together."

Neal grabbed her hand and held it tight. "Then set a date for the wedding."

Angie shrank back. "I need more time," she whispered hoarsely.

"How much time? Six months? A year? I don't care. But I need a definite commitment from you."

She waved her hand in his face. "I'm wearing your ring. Isn't that commitment enough?"

"No, it isn't. Not when you disappear into outer space, the way you've done this weekend. You either want me or you don't. Or maybe you're still holding out for Willis." He knew Willis hovered over their relationship like a dark thundercloud. Sometimes Neal forgot about him, but in moments like these he was only too aware of his glowering presence.

"No, no," Angie said vehemently. "It's over between me and Willis. How many times do I have to tell you that? Why do you keep bringing him up?"

"Because he's there. Between us, Angie, like a wedge."

"I can't undo the past."

"No, but you can stop living in it." He got up abruptly and yanked his coat from the closet by the front door. "I'd like to set a date for our wedding or break the engagement. I can't go on in this limbo. I'll talk to you tomorrow." He opened the door and was gone.

The sound of the door closing echoed in Angie's ears. Her rational mind urged her to hurry down the hall after him, shouting that she would set their wedding date. But she didn't. She sank back into the couch and started to cry, tears of confusion and anger.

When her mind was clear, she could see a wonderful life with Neal, cozy and charming and caring. But at moments like these, the part of her that demanded passion and excitement cried out to be satisfied. That was the part of her Willis appealed to. She had to admit that he had never completely satisfied her emotional needs, for even at his most abandoned he held part of himself in reserve. However, she also knew that he had come closer to that important, deeply hidden part of her than Neal ever could. When she was with Willis, she had given herself up to him completely—heart, body, and soul. And she had gotten back moments of intense and moving emotion. But never more than moments.

Luminous as those moments had been, could they make up for Willis's distance, his impetuousness, his cruelty? She had no illusions about him, but she still craved him. He was a dangerous addiction, no different from drugs or alcohol. Something she would never get over. Something she would have to learn to live with. Or without.

On Monday morning, Neal got to the office early. By dawn he had given up the pretense of trying to sleep and had stared at a session of a televised chemistry course until it was time for the building staff to be opening up at Frame Enterprises. Once in his office, he had gone directly to the drafting table, but he had sketched little but doodles that looked like a host of angels.

Shortly after eight, Robert Delaney, Neal's boss and friend, arrived at work. He noticed that Neal was already bent over his drafting table and went in to say good morning. "Still puzzling over the heating ducts on the Goodman job?" he asked, peering over Neal's shoulder.

Neal put down his pen. "I haven't gotten very far, as you can see."

"Something the matter? You look a bit haggard, and I doubt that you've been losing sleep over heating ducts."

Neal grinned mirthlessly. "Not quite."

"Angie?" Robert ventured.

"What else?"

Robert clapped him on the shoulder. "Let's get a pot of coffee going and have a chat—before hell breaks loose at nine. Come into my office, and bring your mug."

Over fresh coffee, the two men talked for a moment about business, but Robert soon brought the conversation around to Neal's personal life. "Did you and Angie have a fight?"

"Not exactly." He explained how Angie had been so preoccupied all weekend, how she consistently avoided setting a date for their wedding. "I think she's still stuck on Willis. She denies it, but I don't believe her. It's not exactly a great basis to start a marriage on."

"No, it isn't." Robert thought to himself that he was a fine one to be giving advice on marriage. His own experiences had been less than stunning successes, but it was always easier to see someone else's problem clearly and objectively. "Maybe you need to get her away from Willis. You know, out of sight, out of mind."

"Out of temptation," Neal added.

"I don't know what it is about Willis and women. If he could bottle his secret he'd be a millionaire. Between you and me and the lamppost, he's not half the man his brother was, but when it comes to the ladies . . ." Robert shook his head. "It beats me."

"Me too, but what do I do about it?"

"Actually, I have a proposition that may interest you. I was going to take you to lunch this week to talk about it. We can still go to lunch, but I might as well tell you now. You know that Frame is opening a new office in Washington, D.C. I'd like you to manage it. We need someone who's a good architect, a good administrator, and a good businessman. I can't think of anyone better for the position."

Neal listened closely as Robert filled him in on the details of the job. Professionally, it was a plum, and it would put him and Angie—if she would go there with him—far away from Willis. "When would you want me there?" he asked, feeling a taut ball of excitement beginning to form inside him.

"Middle of May, beginning of June at the latest. Would that be too soon?"

"Sounds great to me."

"Then you accept? Of course, this will have to be cleared through the usual channels, but I can't see any problems."

Neal rose and held out his hand. "I accept. And thank you, Robert. I'll never be able to repay you for all you've done for me."

Robert stood and took Neal's hand firmly. "Your success is reward enough."

Neal left Robert's office and hurried back to his own. He rang Angie's desk, even though it was not yet nine. But she was there. "I'm sorry about yesterday," he began. "Can we have lunch? I want to talk to you, and I have some great news."

"I'm sorry, too," Angie said. "How about twelve o'clock?" Neal agreed, and she asked about his news.

"I'm going to keep you in suspense," he said, almost jauntily.

Neal's spirits rose throughout the morning. He was feeling so confident, he reserved a table at Tony's Tavern for lunch.

Angie was surprised when he showed up at her desk with his coat on. "Aren't we going to the cafeteria?"

"Nope. Not today."

Tony's was a former speakeasy that hadn't changed much since Prohibition days. It was dimly lighted, with square wooden tables carved with the initials of hundreds of patrons, oval-bottomed barroom chairs, and sawdust on the floor. The beer was served ice cold in heavy glass pitchers, and the steaks were the best in town.

"This is an unexpected treat," Angie said as they were seated in a booth in the quiet back room, away from the ruckus at the bar. "You'd better tell me that news or you're going to burst."

Neal described the job in glowing terms. "But

the job isn't the best part. It can be the start of a new life for us, Angie. I'd ask to have you transferred there as my administrative assistant. We could go to work together every morning, be together all day. I can see it as clearly as if it were happening right this minute. Will you go with me? I'll try to understand if you can't, but I know this is right for us. I can feel it."

"When do you have to be there?" she asked quietly.

"Middle of May, early June." The knot of tension inside him coiled itself tighter and tighter. Angie was looking down at the table. She took a long time before answering.

"Then why don't we get married the first week in May?" she said finally.

The tight coil inside him sprang loose, filling him with a rush of excitement. "Do you mean that?"

"I'm willing to go to the telephone right now and call my mother. There'll be no turning back after that."

Neal took a quarter from his pocket and put it on the table, and they both burst into joyous laughter. Neal motioned to the waiter and ordered a pitcher of the best draft beer and two filets mignon. They toasted each other and their marriage and the new job with long swallows of icy beer.

Suddenly Neal turned serious. "What made you change your mind?"

Angie explained what had happened on Friday and how she had realized that Willis was an addiction with her. "If I were an alcoholic, I wouldn't try to hide it from you. Why should I try to hide this? I want to lick this addiction, Neal, but I'll need your love to help me."

He reached for her hands and clasped them between his. "You have it. Unconditionally and forever."

Angie was overcome with gratitude and relief. She felt an outpouring of emotion for Neal greater than anything she'd ever had with him. "I love you," she whispered.

Neal's eyes stung with tears. "That's the first time," he said in a choked voice, "you've ever said that to me."

"But not the last time," Angie replied, fully believing that she spoke the truth.

The week that began so auspiciously for Angie and Neal wore Carol to a frazzle. Since the previous Friday she had been waiting for the other shoe to drop. Vic knew about Willis's grandstand play with the Jamison & Pratt deal, but he'd said nothing to Willis or to her—nor, apparently, to anyone else.

In the meantime, she had had to modify the designs for the project. The only way Willis could recoup the money that was going under the table to Bill Jamison was to cut costs. As a consequence, the building would not be the one she had envisioned. That was the thing that really irked her. Because of Willis's insistence on keeping control of the project, she had been forced to do work that was below her standards. The changes she had made weren't dangerous, but the building was less than perfect. She felt sick to her stomach every time she thought of it.

By five o'clock that Wednesday she could work no more. She put her tools away and brought out the brandy bottle—the one she had bought on Monday. It was almost empty. She downed a glass quickly and waited for the spreading warmth to provide its small measure of comfort. Before the brandy had a chance to work, Willis came in.

"I've been over the numbers again," he announced without preliminaries. "You're going to have to cut out some more extras."

"No," she refused flatly. "If I cut out anything else, you might as well forget building these apartments for Jamison and Pratt. You'll have to sell them to the city for low-cost housing."

"Very funny," Willis said with a sneer.

"I wasn't trying to be funny. It's the truth."

"Come on," Willis coaxed. "I've been over the plans. There are a lot of things we can still cut out. Parquet floors, the under-the-counter freezer units, one oven instead of two."

"Sit down, Willis." Carol patted the sofa next to her. He sat down, and she loosened his tie and unbuttoned his top collar button. She kissed him provocatively and felt him respond. It was like a tonic for her, knowing she had power over his body. "Let's talk about this sensibly." As she ran her hands over his chest, she felt his arms tighten around her.

"If you keep this up, we won't be talking about anything, sensibly or not." He cupped the back of her head with his hand and crushed his lips to hers. Minutes later, they both sat back, breathless.

"Now, what did you want to talk about?" Willis asked lazily.

"Jamison and Pratt is getting out of hand. We're going to end up building a lousy building. We're all going to lose our shirts—you, me, Jamison."

"You're starting to sound like a broken record, Carol. Broken records bore me."

Carol ignored his comment. "I think we should cut our losses. Hand the whole thing over to Hastings and let him worry about it. I'm tired of worrying about it. I'm tired of ruining my own work. The construction supervisors do enough damage without me undermining myself. I hate doing shoddy work."

"That's what this is all about, isn't it? You don't care about me or my feelings or getting control of Frame Enterprises. All you care about is your work, whether or not Carol Lamonte is going to look good to the architecture world."

"I still have some integrity left," she answered coolly.

Willis snorted. "I see the moral high horse is out of the barn. May I remind you, before you say anything further about integrity, that you were a willing partner in this venture from the beginning."

"I was a willing partner in a particular plan. It didn't work out the way we expected. I want to drop it and go on to the next thing."

"Fine. You do that." He got up and started for the door. "See you around, baby. It was fun while it lasted."

Carol grabbed him by the arm. "You can't walk out on me."

"Can't I? Just watch me."

She let go of his arm and watched him go to the door. *He's bluffing,* she thought. *He'll turn around.* But when he didn't, she rushed to him.

"Don't go, Willis. We can work this out." She needed him, needed his energy, his drive, his rough brand of loving. She wasn't about to let him walk out on her.

"I won't drop Jamison and Pratt," he said.

"Okay," she relented. "In for a dime, in for a dollar," she said with a sigh.

"That's my baby," he said, lifting his finger to her chin. "You'll get to work on those plans?"

She nodded, silencing the nagging voice inside.

"Good." He lowered his hand from her face, letting it graze her blouse. "There's just one more problem we have to solve." He loved having

Carol on the defensive. He relished the challenge of her, but he also liked knowing he usually had the edge.

"What's that?"

He sat down on her tall drafting stool and hooked his feet on the top set of rungs. "We need to enlist an ally. Sir Galahad really put one over on us with Sloane. I'd like to return the favor."

Carol stood beside her drafting table, facing Willis. If they were going to stay in this game together, they might as well make the smartest moves. "I agree," she said. "Every time I think about Pam Sloane I do a slow burn. One small consolation, though, is that we know where Harvey Blanchard's loyalties really lie."

"A very small silver lining. From now on we trust no one unless we're sure we can control them."

"Which means we'll have to bring in someone from the outside."

"Not necessarily. We have the perfect candidate right here." He paused for effect. "Angie."

"Isn't she leaving soon to marry Neal Johnson? When she goes, we'll be back in the same boat."

"I think," Willis began slyly, "I know a way to keep her from marrying him."

Carol's response was acid. "Isn't that going beyond the call of duty?"

"It won't mean anything, baby, just a way of ensuring that you and I get what we want."

LOVE PLAY

She knew she had lost an important round.
"Willis Frame, you're a wicked son-of-a—"

"And you love me for it," he broke in. He
reached for her, silencing her with a hard,
demanding kiss.

Chapter Eleven
Hopes Raised

Willis went right to work on Angie Perini. He called her into his office at least twice a day, stood close to her, "accidentally" brushed her arm, her hip with his hand. He brought up things they had done together, told her how much he had enjoyed them, told her he thought about them often—and about her. To his surprise her response wasn't immediate, which made his pursuit of her that much more demanding. By the end of the week, though, her resistance was wearing down. He caught her looking at him when she thought he wouldn't notice. The looks were speculative, but only one step short of longing. The time was right for him to make his move.

Friday afternoon, he watched Angie leave the office with Neal. Several hours later he stationed himself in his car outside Angie's apartment building. Not too long after that, Angie and Neal showed up. Willis had a hunch that she never spent the night at Neal's place, and that he never spent the night at hers; he probably brought her home, kissed her chastely, and went home for a cold shower. Willis had no compunctions about horning in on a man like that. In fact, it would be a positive pleasure.

Sure enough, Neal came out of the building about twenty minutes later. Willis waited about ten more minutes—long enough for Angie to start to get ready for bed—and entered the building. He went up to Angie's apartment and knocked on the door.

"Who is it?" Angie called warily.

"It's me. Willis."

Inside the apartment, Angie tightened her robe around her. She wouldn't let him in, that was all there was to it. She went to the door. "Go away, Willis." He didn't respond. "Please."

Willis smiled to himself when he heard her say "please." He'd be inside in a moment or two. "I just want to talk to you."

"About what?"

"I can't tell you through a closed door, Angie. It's late. I'll wake all your neighbors."

She opened the door a crack. "I don't have anything to say to you," she whispered. "Now go away."

"Five minutes. That's all I want. Then I'll go."

A tug-of-war was going on inside Angie. One side of her wanted to pull the door open, the other wanted it shut. Gradually the side that wanted it shut weakened, weakened no matter how hard she resisted. She opened the door.

Willis was ready. He rushed in, closed the door behind them with his heel, and pulled Angie into his arms. He kissed her hungrily and then suddenly let her go, so suddenly he had to grab for her elbow to keep her from stumbling. "For a solid week I've been burning to do that. I've been obsessed with you, Angie. I can't think of anything else."

Her whole body felt as if it were on fire, but she made her words cold. "You can think about me all you want, but don't touch me again. Ever."

"Don't say that," he said desperately. "I couldn't stand it. I was wrong about us, Angie. I thought it was over, I convinced myself it was, but I can't forget you."

Angie broke away and turned her back on him. "You have to forget me. I'm marrying Neal and leaving Bay City. I won't be back."

"You can't leave. I won't let you."

"Don't do this to me," she pleaded.

He came up behind her, put his arms around her waist, and buried his face in her hair. He lifted her hair and kissed the back of her neck over and over, gratified to feel her start to melt in his arms. "I'm so sorry if I hurt you, Angie. So very sorry."

Angie straightened and wriggled out of his grasp, turning to face him. "You tossed me aside. You threw me away like a child does with an old broken toy. You wanted the new, shiny toy. I'm not a plaything."

"I know that," he said contritely. "I was dazzled by Carol at first, but now I've found out how hard and unyielding that shiny surface is. She hasn't got your warmth, your gift for giving. She brings out the ruthlessness in me. I admit I liked it at first. You know what power does to me." He shuddered as if disgusted by his own weakness. "I'm through with her. I need *you*, Angie, to smooth the rough edges, to keep me honest." He looked down and rubbed at his eyes, as if to fight an onslaught of unmanly tears.

Angie felt so sorry for Willis, always buffeted by his own worst instincts, hating himself for his failings. A warning voice told her that was his problem, not hers. But it was not in her nature to see another person suffer and refuse to offer some comfort. "You can do that for yourself. You don't need me." But she didn't believe what she was saying. It was only a halfhearted attempt to keep from succumbing to him.

"Yes, I do," he cried. He pulled her to him again and pressed against her. His breath started to come faster. "I need you. I want you." He reached up and parted her robe, slipping one hand inside to feel her silky nightgown beneath. "I want you now. And tomorrow and the next day and the next." His moment had come. He scooped her into his arms and carried her toward the bedroom.

Angie was beyond resisting. She was free,

flying, intoxicated, invincible. Nothing mattered but holding on to that feeling. Life was a pale shadow; only Willis's wanting her had color and light. In his arms that color and light became a shattering, blinding brightness that blotted out the rest of the world. . . .

The next morning, Angie awoke with a start. Willis was propped on one elbow, looking down at her. For a moment, she was scared. She thought she was having a bad dream, but then she remembered what had happened in the night. She sank back against the pillow, trying to bring herself out of the shadows. Then Willis kissed her and the shadows faded, and the light grew hot and intense once more.

Afterward, Willis moved in for the kill. "Stay with me," he said. "I need you. We belong together." He knew exactly what he was doing, but he genuinely wanted her, too. When he told her how warm and giving she was, it had been a line, but last night had reminded him how soft she was. She was a welcome, exciting change from Carol. "You're not really going to marry Johnson, are you?" he asked, teasing, petulant, but with a note of pleading, too.

"No." How could she marry Neal now? Even if she never saw Willis again, she would always long for him. She could never be a truly faithful wife to Neal, and he deserved better than that. "I'll tell him this morning that I'm calling it off."

Willis smiled happily. "I guess you can't make it any sooner than that."

As soon as Willis left, with promises to call her that afternoon and see her that night, she called Neal and said she needed to see him immediately. He said he'd come right over, but she insisted they meet at a nearby café. She couldn't let him come into the apartment after she'd spent the night there with Willis. She wanted to protect Neal as much as she could; what she had to tell him would be painful enough.

When she went to the mirror to put on her makeup she noticed that her eyes sparkled, her cheeks were flushed, her lips swollen. She looked beautiful, excited, exciting. She tried to cover the glow with makeup, but the feeling came from within. It was too strong to stifle.

Angie was already sipping a cup of coffee in the crowded café when Neal joined her. He greeted her with a kiss and pulled a chair close to hers. "You look great."

Angie lowered her eyes with shame, and bit her lip to keep from crying. She was about to do one of the hardest things she'd ever done in her life—break the heart of a good and decent man who wanted nothing more than the privilege of loving her. She wished desperately that were a privilege she still could bestow, but there was no use kidding herself. She had relinquished that privilege to Willis the night before.

"Did I say something wrong?" He reached under her chin and lifted her face to his, but she quickly averted her eyes. "Hey, what's up, Angie? Is something the matter?"

She couldn't postpone the pain for either of them any longer. She pulled her engagement ring off her finger and slid it across the table. "I can't marry you," she said, still not looking at him.

"What the devil is going on here?" He stared down at the ring, unable, unwilling to touch it. "What do you mean, you can't marry me?"

"I'm sorry. It won't work."

"Last night everything seemed to be working fine. Did this sudden revelation come to you in a dream?" he asked angrily, struggling to keep his voice down. So that's why she had insisted on meeting here; so he wouldn't be able to make a scene. He grabbed the ring and then her arm. "I'm not going to be polite about this, Angie. We'd better get out of here." He threw a bill on the table and hustled Angie out of the café. "I know an absolutely private place where we can talk." He held her arm firmly and walked her to his car.

Angie got into the passenger's side meekly. She had only been trying to spare herself by insisting they meet in the café. There was no reason for Neal to allow her even that much quarter. When Neal was seated beside her she said, "I'd give anything not to have to hurt you, but it's better we split up now. I thought I could make a life with you, but I know now I'd never be the wife you deserve."

"Why? Because you once had an affair with

Willis? If I've told you once I've told you a dozen times: forget the past."

"It's not the past anymore, Neal."

Reeling from the blow, he gripped the steering wheel tightly. "He got to you," he said bitterly. "That lousy, stinking pig got to you."

"He needs me."

"Sure, he needs you," Neal scoffed. "I don't know what for, but I know it will suit his purposes to a tee. Can't you see how he uses you? Angie, Angie, why do you let him do this to you?"

"Because I love him."

"No, you don't," he burst out, "you love me! You told me you love me."

"I slept with him." She knew it was cruel to speak so bluntly, but she had to make Neal see that there was no turning back for her now.

"I don't care about that. I only care—"

"You may say you don't care, but think about how you'd feel on our wedding night, knowing I had been with Willis, measuring yourself against him."

"Shut up!" he shouted. Ashamed by his outburst, he shut his eyes and took a deep breath to calm himself. "What I will show you on our wedding night," he said in even, measured words, "is tenderness, gentleness, true caring."

"There can't be a wedding night." Tears rolled freely down her cheeks. "I know what I'm giving up, but please, please, Neal, let me go. Don't make this any harder than it already is."

"What do you want me to do? Shake hands

and say, 'It's been nice knowing you, have a good life'? You won't get rid of me that easily. Let's give it one more chance. In Washington we can start over. I know it."

She brushed her tears away with the back of her hand. "We can't spend our whole lives starting over." She reached for the door handle. "There's nothing else to say. I'm going."

"At least let me drive you home."

"I'll walk," she said. "It's not far."

He looked at her beseechingly.

"Forget me. Forget you ever met me."

He averted his gaze without a word.

"Good-bye, Neal." She got out of the car and shut the door quietly.

He sat in the car for a long time, numb and drained of all feeling. He was aware of his heart beating, but the rest of his body seemed to have stopped functioning altogether. He didn't know how long it was before he started noticing things again. First it was a smell, her perfume lingering on the icy air. Then he heard her voice saying good-bye, the word echoing in his empty brain. He finally realized what it meant. He rested his forehead on the steering wheel and wept.

When he was finally out of tears, he drove very carefully to his house, not trusting his body to perform even the automatic movements of driving. He went straight to the telephone and called Robert Delaney at home. "I want to leave for Washington as soon as possible." He explained the situation in a tightly controlled, emotionless voice. Robert was understanding and sympathetic and told him to go as soon as he could clear his desk and get his affairs in order.

Neal picked up his briefcase. If he worked around the clock that weekend, he could finish up his outstanding projects at the office. He wouldn't have to go in on Monday and risk seeing her. Then he could pack up and be gone.

He went out to his car and started for the office, but found himself at the park instead, at the edge of the field where he and Angie had walked and played so many times. Winter was dying; the land desperately longed for spring. The earth was a soupy brown, dotted with dirty patches of unmelted snow. But when Neal looked at the field he saw it covered with a canvas of pure clean white, broken only by the outlines of two snow angels.

Angie didn't go home when she left Neal in his car. She couldn't stand the thought of hanging around in her apartment, waiting for Willis to call. She would go right to him. She began to walk, heading clear across town for the luxury apartment building where Willis kept a penthouse apartment. The weather was raw and damp, but she didn't mind the sting of the wind on her cheeks or the painful cold that crept deep into her fingers. She hated hurting Neal as she had, but she was relieved that she had broken the engagement. She could never have lived up to Neal's expectations—of her, or of their marriage.

It would never have been the peaceful haven she once had hoped for. She might have been able to pretend for a while, but sooner or later she would have tired of playing house. No, marriage to Neal would never have been as good as the fantasies she'd had about it. Reality—and that meant Willis—would have set in sometime.

Willis really did need her more than Neal did. Neal could stand on his own; he was strong. Willis needed her to save him from himself. Without her, he would go on acting like a two-year-old, intent on testing his own power by knocking over a pile of blocks. With her at his side he could harness his incredible energy and put it to constructive uses.

By the time she reached Willis's building she had put the ugly scene with Neal behind her. She had begun to imagine how different it would be this time with Willis. She would make him see that it was easier to cooperate with people than it was to ruin them. She would be so loving and understanding that he would bring her all his problems. She would become his closest confidante, and he would become hers.

The doorman on duty recognized Angie from the days when she used to visit Willis. She gave him a friendly smile and said, "Mr. Frame is expecting me. There's no need to ring." He tipped his cap and she hurried to the elevator bank.

* * *

On the top floor of the building, in Willis's bedroom, Carol was listening to Roger Townsend practicing Liszt. Roger was an ambitious graduate student at the Bay City Conservatory. Willis had met him at a party where Roger was picking up a few bucks playing cocktail music. With his unerring nose for a bargain, Willis had befriended Roger. In time he had acquired a full-time valet in exchange for an unused guest room and practice time on Willis's concert grand. Roger had turned out to be an excellent cook and a tenacious watchdog.

Carol had spent the night at Willis's, knowing full well she would spend it alone. Unless something unexpected stopped him, Willis would be spending the night with Angie. And so he had. But she had wanted to be there when he returned, to remind him that it was on her sufferance that he had been with Angie. He had tried to pretend to her that the night with Angie had been a bore, but Carol knew Willis well enough to know when he had enjoyed himself in bed.

She had pretended to be taken in, had gloated with him over Angie's intention to break her engagement. Then she had sent Willis on a wild-goose chase, claiming she had left the Jamison & Pratt plans in the office. When he called from the office because he couldn't find them, she sent him to look for them at her home.

Carol knew that Angie should have broken her engagement by now and ought to be on her way to tell Willis the good news. If she didn't show up, Carol would have to wait for another opportunity to arise. But she hoped she wouldn't have to wait. She wanted to retain the upper hand in this situation, not have to win it back.

Hardly a minute later the doorbell rang. Roger's concentration must have been thrown, for he made a rare error. He broke off for a second, then went back over and played the passage through. The doorbell rang again. Carol heard Roger leave the music room and walk down the hall. She disheveled her hair and disarranged her negligee, then went to stand behind the open bedroom door, ready to make her entrance the moment her cue came.

When Angie first heard the music through the door she thought it was a recording, but when she heard an error and a repeated phrase, she realized someone must be playing Willis's grand piano. She wondered who it could be. Certainly not Willis. He loved music, but he couldn't play more than "Chopsticks." The door opened to reveal a slender young man with close-cropped sandy hair and a pencil-thin moustache.

"Was that you playing? It was beautiful," Angie complimented him.

"Thank you," Roger replied, but his tone was ungracious. The woman's unexpected arrival had caused him to make an error. There was no need to be polite. "Can I help you?"

She was put off immediately by the man's

officious tone. "Is Willis in? I've come to see him."

"About what, madam? He's not in."

Madam, indeed, she thought to herself. "It's a personal matter, and not any business of yours. Who are you?"

Roger bristled. "I'm Mr. Frame's valet."

Angie began to laugh. "His valet!" She'd never figure out where Willis got his ideas. She noticed that the young man was distinctly miffed by her mirth. "I'm sorry to laugh, but I had no idea Willis had a valet. I'm Angie Perini, a close personal friend. I'll just come in and wait for him."

He barred the door. "I'm sorry, madam, but I wasn't told to expect you. I can't let a complete stranger in the house without Mr. Frame's permission."

"Don't be so starchy. It's fine, really." She started to walk past him, but he stopped her forcibly. "Let go of me," she cried.

Carol had just heard her cue. "What's the problem, Roger?" she called as she hurried down the hall.

He kept his hand on Angie's arm. "This person says she's a friend of Mr. Frame's, but I wasn't told—"

"Unhand that maiden," Carol said with a theatrical laugh, noting Angie's shocked expression. "Go back to your practicing. Ms. Perini is perfectly harmless."

Roger inclined his head. "Excuse me."

"Come in, Angie," Carol said with breezy cordiality as she ushered her into the foyer. "I'm terribly sorry. Roger takes his duties a bit too seriously from time to time. If you had let us know you were coming . . ."

"I didn't know I was coming myself," Angie said with difficulty, keeping her eyes on the marble floor. She didn't know where else to look. Even without looking, though, she was all too aware of the lush body beneath Carol's filmy peignoir. Carol had obviously spent the night in Willis's apartment, even though he had told Angie he was finished with Carol. Unless he didn't know she was in his apartment. But then where was he? Hadn't he come back to his apartment after he left her? There had to be some explanation. She would stay until she found out what it was. "Do you know when Willis will be back?" she stammered.

"I'm surprised he isn't with *you*. I understood he was going to spend the night with you. Is there something I can help you with?"

There was the explanation, Angie thought. She'd been made a fool of, not only by Willis but by Carol, too. "No," she said tonelessly. "You've done enough." She stumbled out the door and punched the elevator call button wildly. She thought she'd only ruined one life today, but she'd been more successful than she could have dreamed. She'd ruined two lives, Neal's and her own. And in less than twenty-four hours. Some feat! Her thoughts flew to Neal. He had been right, so very right. She only hoped it would be some satisfaction to him when he found out.

Carol closed the door behind Angie and leisurely strolled to the music room. "I'm sorry to bother you again, Roger." She went to the piano, leaned over the keyboard, and inserted a bill between two keys. "You needn't mention the visitor to Willis."

Roger eyed the bill and smiled blandly at Carol. "What visitor?"

The house was humming with activity and Alice felt almost happy, for the first time since her husband's disappearance. She had only to look at her brother Russ to know that he was overflowing with happiness, and she had gained a new closeness with her sisters-in-law. A new family circle had formed, with one very noticeable gap, but a circle nonetheless.

Alice made the rounds of the house, checking to see that everything was in order for the party she was giving that evening to announce Russ and Sharlene's engagement. The florist was arranging the last of the bouquets in the living room. In the dining room, the caterer's staff was setting up silver chafing dishes and wrapping place settings of silver in crisp linen napkins for the buffet supper that would be served after the champagne toast. In the kitchen, the chef and her assistants were preparing trays of canapés and finishing preparations for the medallions of veal with mushrooms and Madeira that would be served as the main course.

Emma had taken refuge from the hubbub—in the pantry. Alice found her there, pastry gun aimed and at the ready, inspecting the elaborate three-tiered cake she'd spent the better part of the weekend baking.

"Don't shoot!" Alice joked. "I'm not armed."

Emma was too absorbed in her task to laugh. "What do you think?" she asked worriedly.

"I think it's perfect. And I also think you should pack up your pistol and go and have a nice relaxing bath."

Emma glanced at her watch. "Is that the time already? Folks'll be arriving in an hour. I'll go right up," she promised, but it would be another half hour before she was satisfied enough with her creation to leave the pantry.

Even though Alice left the pantry door open when she left, Emma didn't notice her brother Willis come in through the kitchen door and steal up the back stairs.

Willis had had an extremely busy weekend. Between Carol and Angie he didn't know if he was coming or going. Carol was running as hot as a thermal spring; Angie as cold as a glacier. Carol, after sending him on that wild-goose chase for the blueprints the day before, had hardly been able to keep her hands off him. Angie, on the other hand, had refused to talk to him or see him, and he couldn't figure out why.

However, when he stole into Alice's back door at seven o'clock on Sunday evening, he had more pressing business to attend to: a heart-to-heart talk with Sharlene. With this Jamison & Pratt deal so touchy, he needed a way to divert Alice, and what better diversion than another of Sharlene's disappearances. He'd never forgiven Sharlene for betraying him, or for having been a prostitute. He had nothing but contempt for his sister's weakness, her talent for becoming a victim. She practically cried out to be taken advantage of, and he was happy to oblige. Ruining Alice's party was icing on the cake.

He made his way down the hall quickly and entered Sharlene's room without knocking. She saw him in the mirror as he came in and shut the door behind him. The shocked, frightened look on her face spurred him on. "Don't be alarmed. It's only me. Your loving brother."

Sharlene knew that Willis had been invited to the party. Now that he and Alice had established a truce there was no reason for him to be excluded. Sharlene had tried to dissuade Alice from inviting him, but her arguments fell on deaf ears. No matter how many times she told Alice that Willis had acquiesced too easily, that he must be up to something, Alice still insisted on giving him the benefit of the doubt. Sharlene had known she would have to see Willis tonight, but only when she was safely surrounded by Russ, Emma, Alice, and fifty guests. Alone with him in her bedroom she was more frightened than she'd ever been.

"What do you want, Willis?" Her mouth was parched and her words were barely above a whisper.

He leaned casually against the door and crossed his arms over his chest. "I wanted to get your permission to invite another guest to the party tonight."

What do you really want? she longed to scream. Instead she forced herself to get a rein on her fear. She replied tartly, with even a hint of defiance. "Then you should ask Alice, not me. She's the hostess."

"This is a very special guest."

"I don't have time for your games."

Willis went on, unperturbed. "He's an old Navy buddy. We had some great times together, used to hit all the bars in San Diego. I wouldn't be surprised if you knew him—in the Biblical sense, that is. But then, of course, you probably don't remember all your johns. No one could be expected to have that good a memory." He gave her a gloating grin. "So you see, sis, it's not your word against mine anymore. Ol' Billy could be here in thirty or forty minutes, max."

"You're bluffing," she stammered uncertainly.

"Want to try me out?"

"Why are you doing this to me?" she cried, her voice sounding strangled and distorted.

"Keep it down," Willis ordered, and took several threatening steps toward her, "unless you want to make this a group interview." He could see Sharlene was getting disoriented and panicky. "I'm doing this because I hate having a sister who's so common and vulgar—"

"And all your lying and cheating is the mark of a true gentleman, I suppose," Sharlene broke in recklessly.

Willis laughed softly. "Oh-ho, the kitten has claws, does she? Well, not for long." He shook his head with feigned regret, and took on an intimate, confiding tone. "You know, I might have been able to forgive you, but then you betrayed me. All I wanted you to do was keep Alice out of my way, but you wouldn't help. You brought all this on yourself. You can't expect any sympathy from me."

"I'll do anything you want, just don't ruin my life," Sharlene pleaded.

"Sorry, kid, it's too late for that."

Sharlene burst into tears. "Then tell him, go ahead and tell Russ. Do it tonight, in front of all the guests. Just get it over with. I don't care anymore."

"In that case, I just might," he mused. "I'd better call Bill and tell him to get over here as soon as possible. I don't suppose Alice would mind another guest. And even if she did, she'd be too polite to say anything. I wonder if she'll be too polite to throw you out of her house."

He scratched his chin thoughtfully and turned to go. "See you later, sis."

Willis checked his watch as he strode into the hall. Seven-fifteen. He'd bet that Sharlene would be out of the house by seven-thirty.

He had just closed the door when Emma stepped out of her room. "What are you doing here?" she demanded fiercely.

"Simmer down, Em. I only came to wish the blushing bride-to-be good luck. I don't know if Sharlene told you, but we've had our differences lately—"

"So I heard," she put in caustically. "I know the whole story, Willis, and believe me, if you do anything more to harm her, I won't rest until you're ruined. I'll swear to that on Mama's Bible."

Willis held up his hands defensively. "Honest, I only came to apologize and wish her all the best. Alice has been so generous to me, I figure I can afford to be generous in my turn."

Emma eyed her brother skeptically. "I'm choosing to believe you for the moment, but if I find out you've lied, you'll live to regret it."

"I guess that means you're going to let me live."

"For the time being." She turned her back on him and marched on down the hall. When she heard Willis go down the back stairs she knocked on Sharlene's door. "It's Emma, honey."

Sharlene called to her to come in.

"I just ran into Willis in the hall," Emma said. "He told me he'd come to bury the hatchet. Is that true?"

At the sound of Emma's voice, Sharlene had bent over at the waist and started brushing her hair up from the nape of her neck. Now she stood up, hoping that Emma would take the color in her cheeks as natural. "He nearly scared me to death, barging in here like a thief, but he really did come to say he was sorry." She had already decided that if anyone saw Willis leaving her room she would tell them that story. Otherwise she would never be left alone long enough to escape.

Emma examined her sister's face carefully. "You've been crying."

"I'm just so relieved, that's all." Sharlene held her hands behind her so that Emma wouldn't see her crossed fingers. It was a childish thing to do, but her life depended on being able to get away before her engagement to Russ was officially announced and toasted. Childish gestures and baldfaced lies were the only weapons she had to fight with.

Emma went to Sharlene and hugged her close. "Go and splash those red eyes with cold water and finish dressing. The doorbell ought to start ringing any minute."

Sharlene let herself lean against her sister for a moment. She hated even the thought of hurting her, but she had no choice. Willis had backed her into a corner again. She pushed herself away from Emma bravely. "I'll be a few minutes," she said. "I want to do my makeup over."

"All right. Alice and I will hold the fort." Emma turned to go but stopped at the door. "Enjoy yourself tonight, honey."

"I will," Sharlene said, barely able to stem her tears. "And thanks for everything."

As soon as Emma left, Sharlene started tossing things in a suitcase. The doorbell began to ring and she heard Emma and Alice greeting the guests. The hum of voices grew steadily louder as she dressed in a dark, inconspicuous pants suit and a nondescript winter coat. When the coast was clear, she hurried down the back stairs and out the kitchen door.

Russ arrived at Alice's feeling as if he were wearing skates instead of shoes. He glided in the front door, where he was greeted affectionately by his sister and his sister-in-law-to-be. He was told Sharlene had had a late attack of nerves and would be down as soon as she redid her makeup. So he rolled smoothly into the living room, where he was greeted like a film star who'd just won an Academy Award. Spinning slowly around the room, he accepted the many handshakes and congratulatory slaps on the back he was offered.

He was having such a good time he didn't realize how fast time was passing. He didn't notice Alice's furtive conferences with the chef or the worried glances she exchanged with Emma. Russ finally noticed the time when Willis joked—rather tastelessly, Russ thought—that he'd never heard of a bridegroom being jilted at the engagement party. It was eight-fifteen. What could be keeping Sharlene? Immediately he began to worry. Could she have had an accident? Was she ill? He excused himself and hurried upstairs.

He found Emma sitting on Sharlene's bed, head in hands. The room was a shambles —drawers turned out, clothes and hangers littering the floor.

"What's happened?" he whispered.

Emma snapped out of her despair, knowing that Russ and Alice would need her to think clearly and act decisively in the next difficult hours. "She's gone, Russ," she said as gently as she could.

"What do you mean, gone?"

"I guess Sharlene's too afraid of happiness. She's run off again."

Russ sank down on the bed beside Emma. "Why is she afraid? What is she afraid of? I've never done or said anything to hurt her."

Emma patted Russ on the shoulder. "I know you haven't. You stay here. I'll go down and tell Alice. I expect she'll want to say that Sharlene's not well and you're looking after her. Is that all right with you?"

"Sure, fine," Russ mumbled. It didn't matter to

him what Alice said or did. People would be gossiping about him, anyway; *Poor Russ Matthews, such bad luck with women.* Emma left, and he stood up and started pacing the room. He couldn't take that happening to him again. He wouldn't let it. He'd find Sharlene, wherever she was, and marry her even if he had to drag her to the altar.

Downstairs, Alice asked for her guests' attention. She told them Sharlene was unwell and invited them into the dining room for supper. As the subdued party filed dutifully to the buffet table, Emma found her brother and took him aside.

Willis followed her to the pantry more or less willingly, but Emma was so angry she would have had no trouble putting him in a headlock and pulling him there by force. She shut and locked the door behind them.

"I thought I was being taken behind the woodshed," Willis said glibly.

Emma faced him with deadly calm. "Don't give me any of your lip. You listen to me and you listen hard. I am going to find Sharlene and get her back here. She is going to marry Russ. You are never going to speak to Sharlene again unless I am in the room. If you do, I will tell Alice all about the time that Steve practically had to put his business in hock to bail you out of that phony land scheme and keep you out of jail. You may have pulled the wool over Alice's eyes, but you haven't pulled it over mine. You step out of line again and I won't rest until I've exposed you for the lying, cheating skunk you are."

"Please stop, Emma, you're getting me all scared," Willis mocked.

Emma raised her hand and slapped him full across the face with all her might. "I mean it." She stalked out of the pantry.

Willis winced and rubbed his stinging cheek. "So I noticed," he murmured to the empty room. As he started to leave, he caught sight of the cake on the counter. He had overheard Alice say that Emma had made it. Too bad she'd done all that work for nothing. There probably wouldn't be anyone around to eat it. He reached out and with one hard sweep of his arm toppled the cake onto the pantry floor.

The guests and caterers were gone. Alice, Emma, and Russ sat in different corners of the room, all lost in private thought. Finally Alice broke the deep, troubled silence that had settled over the living room. "I still don't understand how the cake could have fallen on the floor."

Emma's temperature soared near the boiling point, but she said nothing. She had no proof, but she had a very strong suspicion about how that cake had ended up on the floor. What a little weasel Willis was!

Several minutes later, Russ asked Alice if he could move some of the flowers out of the living room. "The smell is getting to me." Actually, the smell reminded him of a funeral parlor, and their gathering, of a sparsely attended wake.

"Do you think we should call the police?" Alice asked after another long pause.

"She has to be missing twenty-four hours before they can do anything," Russ replied glumly.

"I'm keeping her in my thoughts," Emma said, "telling her to call me. I think she will. We'll just have to sit tight."

And so it went until well after midnight. The ring of the telephone passed through the room like a jolt of electricity. Emma sprang up and made for the hall, the others fast on her heels. She picked up the phone.

"It's her," she mouthed to Alice and Russ. She kept trying to break in, but without success. When she finally had a chance to speak, the line went dead. She replaced the receiver. "Of course she begged me not to tell you, but I have to. She's in San Francisco at the Russian Hill Hotel. She said to apologize to you both."

Alice sagged against the table in relief. Russ put his arm around his sister's shoulder and kissed her on the cheek. He reached for Emma's hand and vowed, "I'm going out to get her, and I'm not coming back until we're married. I can't take this anymore."

As Russ hurried out the door, Emma put Sharlene in her thoughts again. *Tell him*, her mind screamed. *Tell him, honey, or you'll never have any peace.* She looked up at Alice. Her usually creamy porcelain skin was white with fatigue and worry. "What we both need is a nice cup of tea, and a good night's rest. There's nothing more we can do tonight."

Alice smiled wearily. "How did I ever manage without you, Emma?"

Russ drove directly to the airport. He caught the red-eye to San Francisco and arrived at the Russian Hill Hotel long before dawn. He amazed the clerk by asking for the best suite they had available, prepaying the bill by credit card, then refusing to see or occupy the rooms. Still in his rumpled tuxedo, he took up a chair in the lobby and sat there through the night, staying awake by reading through a pile of magazines, word for word, cover to cover. Every two seconds he looked up to see if Sharlene had come into the lobby.

In her modest single room on the hotel's eighth floor, Sharlene was tossing and turning. Running away wasn't the answer. What was she going to do in San Francisco? Find a job, carve out a life for herself until Willis caught up with her, then run somewhere else? Emma was right. She had to face up to her past or she'd never have a future. She battled her fears, fighting for the courage to return to Bay City, to take the chance of losing Russ by telling him the truth.

By dawn, she had won enough of a victory to dress and go downstairs. She would check out of the hotel, take a taxi to the airport, and fly home. Home. It had been a long time since she'd had a home. Now she knew she did, and that she belonged there.

She stepped off the elevator and into the lobby, concentrating intently on holding on to her resolve and determination. Suddenly she heard her name. A figure in black and white rushed to her and embraced her. She was so surprised it took her a moment to realize it was Russ. As soon as she did, she threw her arms around him.

"Are you all right?" he asked frantically.

"Now I am. I thought I was being attacked by a mad penguin."

He threw back his head and laughed without reservation, feeling all the stress and tension fly away. Everything was going to be all right, just as soon as they got married. He'd better get the ball rolling. The plain black pants suit Sharlene was wearing would not do at all. He hustled her into the elevator. "Did you bring anything else to wear?"

"A few things," she replied, puzzled.

Once inside her room, he went through the things she'd brought and picked out a simple cream-colored shirtwaist dress. "Go put this on," he ordered. "Don't ask any questions, just do it." When Sharlene came out of the bathroom he went in—and left the door open while he washed his face, rubbed some toothpaste over his gums with his finger, and combed his hair.

Except for Russ's ebullient mood, Sharlene

might have felt apprehensive, but she went along with him docilely. After all, his being there had just saved her hours and hours of keeping hold of her courage.

"Ready?" he asked when he emerged from the bathroom.

"I guess so." She couldn't imagine what he was up to. When they got outside the hotel and Russ asked the doorman to hail a taxi, her curiosity got the better of her. She asked him where they were going.

"To City Hall. We're getting married as soon as the ink is dry on the license," he answered firmly. "I don't want to hear any *ifs*, *ands*, or *buts*. I only want to hear *I do*s." He took her in his arms and kissed her deeply. "I love you, Sharlene. I want to make sure you don't ever leave me again."

"I won't, Russ. I promise," she replied. "But there's something I have to tell you. Something that happened to me awhile ago, something I've been trying to run away from."

Russ silenced her with a finger on her lips. "I don't want to hear it. Nothing could stand in the way of my loving you."

It would have been so easy to stop right there, but Sharlene made herself go on. "I can't marry you unless I tell you. It wouldn't be fair."

"The only thing that wouldn't be fair is if you didn't marry me. I'm telling you, I don't care about the past, Sharlene. I care about the future. Yours and mine. Together." He pulled from his pocket a box that contained the wedding ring he had bought for Sharlene. "I meant to give you this last night, but it gives me no less pleasure to give it to you now."

Sharlene looked down at the beautiful diamond-encrusted ring, and her resolve crumbled irrevocably. She had tried, honestly tried to tell Russ the truth, but he didn't want to hear it. "I'll be the best wife I can to you, Russ. I love you."

She said nothing more until she was repeating her wedding vows.

By noon Dr. and Mrs. Russell Matthews were installed in their suite in the Russian Hill Hotel. A champagne brunch had been ordered and was on its way. Sharlene, radiant with happiness, wanted to share her joy.

"Can we call Emma and Alice?" she asked.

He answered by dialing his sister's number. When it started to ring he handed the phone to Sharlene.

Alice picked up the phone on the first ring, taking Sharlene by surprise. "It's me. Sharlene," she stammered. After the first words the rest came easily—her embarrassed apologies for deserting the party, and then the news that she and Russ were married. Alice, overjoyed, called Emma to the phone and Sharlene repeated the whole story.

"I suppose you and Russ had a long talk and got *everything* straightened out," Emma said to her.

Alice must be standing nearby, Sharlene thought. She lowered her voice. "No, not *every-*

thing," she replied, emphasizing the word the way Emma had. "I tried hard, but he wouldn't listen to me."

There was a pause, and she heard Emma sigh. Then Emma wished her all the happiness in the world and asked to speak to Russ.

Sharlene sat motionless while her husband talked to Emma and then Alice. The memory of Emma's heartfelt sigh echoed loudly in her ears.

Back in Bay City, Alice was as giddy as a schoolgirl. "I do believe this calls for a celebration," she said. "There just happen to be a few bottles of chilled champagne in the house . . ."

"Champagne?" Emma exclaimed. "In the middle of the day? Oh, why not?" She pushed away the dark thoughts occasioned by the news that Sharlene hadn't told Russ the truth. She did believe that Sharlene had tried, but how hard? On the other hand, if Russ didn't want to hear her out, what could she do?

Alice started for the kitchen, but Emma insisted on getting the wine herself. "Maybe I'll heat up some of those leftover canapés while I'm at it. We wouldn't want to get too tiddly, would we?" She hurried into the kitchen, quickly popped a tray of hors d'oeuvres in the oven, and picked up the phone. The food was only an excuse to give her time to pass on the news to Willis.

* * *

When the receptionist buzzed to tell Willis that his sister Emma was on the line, he debated about whether or not to take the call. Finally he answered with a cautious hello. He would see what Emma had to say before deciding on his next move.

"I've got some good news and some bad news," Emma started right in. "The good news is that Russ and Sharlene got married this morning. The bad news is that what I said last night still holds, especially after what you did to my cake, you weasel!"

Willis smirked to himself, but replied contritely. Chalking up a few points with Emma couldn't do any harm. "I'm really sorry about the cake," Willis replied humbly. "I don't know what got into me. It was a cruel and childish thing to do."

"It certainly was," Emma agreed. Still, she was somewhat mollified. Willis rarely offered apologies or admitted his mistakes. "And I'm glad to hear you say it. I just hope you've come to your senses about Sharlene, too. She's been through so much, Willis. Let her have a chance at happiness. It's no skin off your nose. Unless of course you choose to ruin her marriage. Then you won't have a nose left to skin."

Willis wanted to crow. Emma had just let slip that Sharlene hadn't told Russ the truth. It was still waiting to be told. For the moment, however, he restrained himself. He had to make Emma think he would do what she wanted him to do. "I know you mean what you say, Emma. You always have," he said, sounding grave and serious.

"And I always will." Emma hung up and reached for one of Alice's best crystal champagne flutes from the cupboard. She had just taken the delicate stem between her fingers when she realized what she'd done. She'd let Willis know that Sharlene hadn't told Russ. How could she have been so stupid? The glass slipped from her hands and shattered into a thousand slivers.

An instant later, Alice hurried into the kitchen. "Are you okay, Emma?"

"I broke a glass," she answered dully. "I'm sorry."

Alice wondered why the small accident seemed to have upset Emma so much. She reached for the dustpan and brush and began to sweep up the debris. "It's only a glass," she said. "I can replace it."

"Yes, I suppose you can," Emma replied, staring down at the sparkling shards. There were thousands of glasses like the one she'd broken, but who was going to replace her sister's dreams when Willis shattered them?

Brunch at the Russian Hill Hotel lived up to its name. First the waiter served Russ and Sharlene a plate of blini—light buckwheat pancakes topped with sour cream and caviar. Then they moved on to chicken Kiev, rice and fresh vegetables, and slices of chocolate raspberry torte for dessert. All accompanied by a bottle of well-chilled champagne.

They ate slowly, savoring the food and the moment, toasting each other throughout the meal. When they had finished eating, Russ poured the last of the wine into their glasses and reached across the table. He entwined his arm with his bride's and raised his glass. "To us, to our love and happiness," he proposed, looking deep into Sharlene's eyes.

"Forever," she added, meeting his gaze.

They drank, more of each other than of the wine. When their glasses were empty, Russ dismissed the waiter from their suite. He took the glass from Sharlene's hand, then rose and held out his hand to help her up. He looked at her with longing and, cupping her face in his hands, kissed her deeply.

"My wife," he whispered. "My precious wife."

"I love you," Sharlene murmured, and pressed against him.

Desire rose in him with the speed and force of a tidal wave. He scooped her into his arms and carried her into the bedroom, stepping swiftly over the threshold of their new life together.

In his office, Willis riffled through the clutter in his top desk drawer, searching for a business card he'd dropped there a few days earlier. After a number of sharp oaths he found it: WILLIAM C. EVANS. BAY CITY ELECTRONICS. 555-3489. He couldn't believe that stroke of luck—running into Billy Evans after all these years since being in the service. With Sharlene and Russ married, any trouble Willis caused them would do more than divert Alice, it would rip her to shreds. Then he'd finally be able to get on with his plans to take over Frame Enterprises.

He picked up the phone and dialed through. "Bill? Willis Frame here. . . . Terrific. How about yourself? . . . Glad to hear it. Look, Bill, there's someone I'd like you to meet. . . ."